"Are you always a pest or do I just bring out the worst in you?"

Donovan only laughed. "Me? A pest? You must be joking. Everyone knows I'm a sweetheart."

"Uh-huh," she said dryly. "And I'm Snow White."

"No, you're Sleeping Beauty. And you know what happened to her."

Confused, she frowned. "The wicked witch got her?"

"No. The prince kissed her until she woke up."

"Oh, no!" she said. "Don't even think about going there, mister. You're no Prince Charming." The second the words were out of her mouth, she knew that she'd made a mistake. He wasn't the kind of man who ignored a challenge.

"Too late," he chuckled, and reached for her. A heartbeat later, she was in his arms.

Dear Reader,

This is the first time I've done a series in which the mystery isn't solved until the end of the fourth book, so I was naturally a little nervous when I started writing *Bounty Hunter's Woman*. There was a lot to bring together, and only a limited number of pages in which to do it. But then Donovan Jones came to Priscilla Wyatt's rescue, and the rest, as they say, is history. I loved the sparks that flew between Donovan and Priscilla. He's a man who can't resist a woman in trouble, and she's up to her ears in bad guys. Donovan thinks she's spoiled and stubborn…and no one's more surprised than he when she turns out to be perfect for him. Don't you just love surprises? Enjoy.

Linda Turner

LINDA TURNER

Bounty Hunter's Woman

Silhouette®

Romantic

SUSPENSE

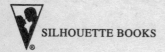

SILHOUETTE BOOKS

Recycling programs
for this product may
not exist in your area.

ISBN-13: 978-0-373-27613-4
ISBN-10:   0-373-27613-3

BOUNTY HUNTER'S WOMAN

Visit Silhouette Books at www.eHarlequin.com

Printed in U.S.A.

LINDA TURNER

began reading romances in high school and began writing them one night when she had nothing else to read. She's been writing ever since. Single and living in Texas, she travels every chance she gets, scouting locales for her books.

Prologue

Moving gingerly, the incision from her surgery twinging in protest, Priscilla Wyatt stepped through the front door of her London flat and found herself blinking back tears. Over the course of the last week and a half, while she was in the hospital recovering from injuries incurred in a car accident and the emergency surgery that had saved her life, she'd begun to wonder if she was ever going to sleep in her own bed again. When her doctor had finally told her she was being released, she hadn't known whether she wanted to laugh or cry.

Watching her as the last of her strength gave out and she sank down onto the couch, her brother, Buck, frowned in concern. "I don't know what the doctor was thinking, releasing you so soon after your surgery. Look at you. You're as weak as a kitten."

"I just need to rest for a few minutes, and I'll be fine."

"Yeah, right," he retorted, scowling. "In case you've forgotten, you had a hell of an accident. You could have been killed—"

Hovering at the door, his wife, Rainey, frowned warningly. "She's aware of that, Buck. You don't have to keep reminding her."

"Apparently, I do," he growled. "She'd still be in the hospital if she hadn't pressured the doctor to release her."

"I can recover better here," Priscilla replied. "No one gets any rest in the hospital. You know that."

"What I know is that you had major surgery. You lost your spleen, dammit. This is serious, Cilla. You've got no business being here by yourself."

"Why don't you come home with me and Buck?" Rainey suggested. "Let us take care of you."

"Oh, no!" she said quickly. "The ranch isn't home. This is. *London* is."

Buck could understand her feelings. When Hilda Wyatt, a distant American relative from the States, had left the Broken Arrow Ranch in Colorado to him and his sisters, the place had felt nothing like home even though it had been in the Wyatt family for nearly a hundred fifty years. That was before the ranch came under attack, however. The first time he picked up a gun to defend the Broken Arrow, the land of his ancestors became his.

Not that he and his sisters could claim it outright just yet, he reminded himself. Hilda had wanted the ranch to go to the last of the Wyatts, but she'd still left it to them with strings. One of them had to be at the ranch at all times for the period of one year. If there was no

Wyatt at the ranch for two nights in a row during that year, they lost the Broken Arrow and it went to an unnamed heir. No one, however, knew who the unnamed heir was. His or her name was in a sealed envelope that would only be opened in the event that the English branch of the Wyatts was disqualified.

And it was that clause in the will that had caused countless problems for him and his sisters, Buck thought in disgust. Once the terms of the will became common knowledge, everyone in Willow Bend seemed to think they were the unnamed heir and all they had to do to inherit the ranch was drive Buck and his sisters away.

The attacks began almost immediately and had been going on for months, always coming from a different direction. And they hadn't stopped at the property lines of the ranch...which was why he and Rainey were in London.

"You're not safe here," he told Priscilla flatly. "Your accident wasn't an accident."

"We don't know that for sure," she argued. "Just because someone ran a stop sign—"

"All the witnesses said the driver could have easily avoided the accident," he cut in. "He didn't. We can't prove it, but my gut tells me the jackass was hired by someone in Colorado to hurt you and draw the rest of us away from the ranch. If that's the case, this is only the beginning. Whoever hired the man who hit you will try again."

When she shivered, hugging herself, he said huskily, "I'm not trying to scare you, Sis. But we're all worried sick about you. You're here alone, and you're so weak you can't possibly protect yourself if someone decides to come after you. If you'd just come home with me and Rainey until you're stronger, I promise I won't say a word to stop you when you're ready to come back here to London. I'll even help you pack."

If her stomach hadn't been in knots at the thought of someone stalking her, trying to hurt her, she would have laughed. "Yeah, right. The second I even bring up the subject of going back to London, I'm going to get grief from the entire family, and you know it."

Not bothering to deny it, he only grinned. "And your point is?"

"You're terrible." She laughed…and gave in. "Okay, I'll go. But don't say I didn't warn you. I *will* go home as soon as I'm feeling better."

"We'll talk about it then." He chuckled and strode over to the phone to call the airline and book their tickets.

Chapter 1

There was, Priscilla decided, nothing like the scent and colors and sounds of harvest. Sitting on the tailgate of the old Ford pickup that was used for work on the ranch, she watched, entranced, as Buck and her soon-to-be brothers-in-law, John and Hunter, cut and baled the alfalfa that had been planted last spring in the lower pastures. A gentle breeze caught the dust from the fields and sent it swirling, and in the long shadows of the late afternoon, the air turned golden.

Wishing she'd brought her camera, Priscilla couldn't remember the last time she'd felt such peace. She'd been at the Broken Arrow for nearly two months, and in all that time, there hadn't, thankfully, been a single attack against the ranch. She'd had time to heal…and to grow to appreciate the land of her American ancestors. And without quite knowing how it had happened, Colorado had become home.

She couldn't, however, stay any longer. She had responsibilities in London she needed to get back to, and she was stunned to realize how much she hated the idea of leaving. How her brother and sisters would laugh when she told them that, she thought ruefully. She'd been the last to leave England, the lone holdout in the family who'd been so positive that she wanted no part of living in the wilds of Colorado. And now just the thought of leaving made her want to cry.

"You're awfully quiet," her sister Elizabeth said as the men called it a day and started across the field toward where the women of the family waited under the lone tree at the edge of the field. "Are you all right? Maybe you should have stayed at the house."

"I'm fine."

"The doctor said you were supposed to take it easy," Katherine reminded her. The closest sister to her in age, Katherine looked just like their mother when she frowned at her in concern.

"It's been two months since my surgery," she replied. "I'm completely healed. Really."

Studying her shrewdly, her sister-in-law, Rainey, said, "The removal of a spleen's not something you get over in a week or two. And you have been helping out a lot around the ranch lately. Maybe you need to pace yourself more."

Joining them in time to hear his wife's comments, Buck shot Priscilla a sharp look. "What's wrong?"

"Nothing," she said. "Everyone thinks that just because I'm not talking much, I'm not feeling well.

I'm fine. I don't need to take it easy. I just have a lot on my mind."

"You want to go back to London, don't you?" Elizabeth guessed, studying her with shrewd blue eyes. "You're homesick."

"She is not!" Katherine retorted before she could answer. "She's still having nightmares about the accident, and she should be. It wasn't an accident! Someone tried to kill her. If I were her, I'd never step foot in England again."

"She has to finish her internship," Rainey reminded Katherine. Turning to Priscilla, she frowned. "I thought you were going to wait until the probation period on the ranch was up, then go back to London after Christmas."

"That was my plan," she admitted. "But I have some things that need to be taken care of now. I can't just keep putting them off."

"No," Buck said firmly.

"I've been paying for a flat that I haven't used for two months," she argued. "And I don't want to be in London anymore. I need to give up the lease, but I can't just abandon my things. I have to go back, make arrangements for movers—"

"You can do that from here," Katherine pointed out.

"True," she agreed, "but I also need to talk to Jean Pierre…"

"So call him," Elizabeth said.

"No, I need to meet with him face-to-face. I'd like to finish my internship from here, if possible, and I'll have a better chance of talking him into that if I can sit down with him and explain my plan."

"You're safer here," Buck insisted. "Wait until after

the ranch is ours and we'll all go back for awhile. I want to show Rainey where we grew up—"

"That's another month," she argued. "And I still don't think my accident was anything but that—an accident!"

"You don't know that."

"Yes, I do! No one's attacked the ranch since I've been here. If someone really tried to get to me in London, why wouldn't they do it here?"

"Because we're all here together," he replied. "No one's going to take on all four of us together. It's when we're apart that we're vulnerable."

"I'm not going back to stay," she pointed out. "I'll just be in London for two or three days at the most. And no one but the family even has to know I'm gone. I'll fly out of Denver in the dead of night. No one will see me leave, and if you casually mention around town that we've all been staying home because a stomach bug has been working its way through the family, no one will suspect a thing."

When he just looked at her, unconvinced, she played her trump card. "You told me in London that if I would come home with you to the ranch to recover, you wouldn't offer a word of protest when I was ready to go back to London. I expect you to keep that promise."

She had him, and they both knew it, but this wasn't about winning points off each other. Over the course of the last eleven months, when they'd inherited the ranch and then found themselves under attack by the faceless enemies who were after the Broken Arrow, the four of them had grown closer than ever. She needed him and her sisters to support her decision and trust her judgment.

"I'll be careful," she told Buck. "I promise."

He hesitated, his eyes searching hers, only to sigh in defeat. "Okay. But you call in every hour once you land just so we'll know you're safe. Understood?"

"Every hour," she promised, hugging him. "I'll be fine. You'll see."

Less than thirty-six hours later, she walked into her flat in London and found it just as she'd left it. Automatically locking the door behind her, she made a quick tour and wasn't surprised to find the plants on her kitchen windowsill dead and the food in her refrigerator molded and sour. She hadn't exactly had time to clean things out before she'd left. The second she'd been released from the hospital, Buck had given her ten minutes to throw some clothes and personal items into a suitcase before he'd rushed her to the airport and the States.

She'd thought about her flat often over the course of the last two months and wondered how she would feel when she returned. Would she be scared? Nervous? Happy to finally be home? Frowning, she realized, she didn't feel any of those things. Instead, the stale air of her flat seemed to close in on her, and she found herself longing for the fresh, clean air of the ranch. Outside, London traffic rushed by, but all she wanted to hear was the low call of the cattle grazing in the pasture and the whisper of the wind through the pines.

Loneliness tugged at her heart, and she almost reached for her phone to call home. But she'd spoken to Buck the second she'd landed. He'd be worried if she called him now—less than thirty minutes later. She had things to do, anyway. She had to pack, notify the landlord that she was moving out, find a place to store her things. But first she had to call a mover.

Settling at the kitchen table with the phone book, she started making calls. She soon discovered, however, that finding the right person for the job—as well as a storage unit she could afford—took longer than she'd expected. Three precious hours later, she finally found a mover who could pick up her furniture by the end of the week. Her lease wasn't up until the following Monday, but she'd hoped to find someone who could come while she was still there to oversee the move. Obviously, that wasn't going to be possible. She'd promised the family that she'd be back in three days, and she was standing by her word. She'd just have to give the key to the landlord and trust him to supervise things. Resigned, she started packing.

Later, she never knew where the rest of the afternoon went. One minute, the sun was high in the sky, and the next time she looked up, the day had given way to the darkening shadows of twilight. Surprised, she glanced around and discovered the flat was littered with dozens of boxes that were packed full of books, dishes, the contents of her kitchen cupboards, not to mention the bathroom and the front closet. And she hadn't even touched her bedroom yet!

Exhausted, she plopped down on the couch. How was she going to get everything packed and still have time to meet with Jean Pierre before she left to fly home? She didn't want to put her internship—and her degree in fashion design—on hold, but what choice did she have? She wasn't safe in London.

Suddenly, without warning, there was a sharp knock

at the door. Startled, she jumped, her heart slamming against her ribs. She wasn't expecting anyone. No one even knew she was there except her family. So who was knocking on her door?

Her blood turning to ice at the possibilities, she hugged herself and sat as quiet as a mouse right where she was. Whoever was on the other side of the door didn't know she was there. When she didn't answer, he would assume no one was home and leave.

"Miss Wyatt? Are you in there? Open up. This is the police. I need to speak to you. I have some bad news about your family in the United States."

"Oh, God!" Panic suddenly squeezing her throat, she jumped up and ran to the door. She reached for the dead bolt, only to hesitate, horrified by a sudden thought. What if this was a trick? What if whoever was after the ranch somehow found out she'd gone back to London? Could they have found out where she was already?

"Who did you say you were?" she asked, wincing at the quiver of fear she clearly heard in her voice. "I need some identification."

"I'm Officer Hastings," he replied and held up his badge to the peephole in the door.

Priscilla took one look at it and sighed in relief. Lightning quick, she flipped the dead bolt and jerked open the door. "Come in—"

She didn't have time to say another word, let alone scream, as two masked men with guns rushed through the door and grabbed her. Gasping, she tried to scream…only to have duct tape slapped over her mouth. Frantic, she clawed at the tape, but they were ready for her. In the next instant, her wrists were taped together, then her ankles. Trussed up like a turkey, there was nothing she could do as they picked her up and laid her on the floor. Before she could even begin to guess their intentions, they rolled her up in the living room rug.

Just that easily, fear took on a new name. Terror.

When Donovan Jones caught his secretary on the phone with her boyfriend for the fifth time in two days, he was in no mood to cut her any slack. He'd already warned her numerous times that she was there to work, not visit with her lover, and she'd completely ignored him. She was the third secretary he'd hired in three weeks…and the third one who seemed to think she could do whatever the hell she wanted. She was wrong.

"You're fired," he growled. And leaning across the desk, he pushed the disconnect button on the phone.

Sputtering, she surged up out of her chair in anger. "What the hell?!"

Not the least bit impressed with her indignation, he growled, "Get your purse and get out. Now! I'll put your paycheck in the mail tomorrow."

He didn't give her time to argue but simply grabbed her purse from where she insisted on leaving it on top of a file cabinet and strode over to the door. Jerking it open, he waited. She was so furious, steam was practically coming out of her ears. Cursing, she jerked her purse out of his hand and stormed out, slamming the door so hard that she nearly knocked it off its hinges.

"Good riddance," he muttered. "I don't need you anyway. I can find my own files."

But when he stalked over to the filing cabinet, the file he needed for a meeting he had scheduled in fifteen minutes wasn't where it should have been. Swearing, he went through the entire drawer to make sure it hadn't been misfiled, but it was nowhere to be found.

Which meant, he thought grimly as his gaze landed on the secretary's desk, it had to be somewhere in the mountain of paperwork that completely covered the top of the desk. She'd been there a week, he thought, irritated. What the hell had she been doing? He'd been on a case and had to leave the office in her hands. Apparently, she hadn't done a damn thing except talk on the phone to her boyfriend.

Next time, he told himself, he was going to avoid the young chicks like the plague and hire a little, old, gray-haired grandmother instead. Someone who would appreciate the job, he decided, and not take advantage of the fact that he was hardly ever in the office. Someone who—

When the outer office door suddenly opened behind him, he stiffened. If the little witch had come back to plead for her job, she could forget it, he thought. She was history. Pivoting sharply, ready to tell her just that, he found himself confronting a stranger, instead.

Frowning—had he forgotten an appointment?—he lifted a dark brow. "May I help you?"

"I'm looking for Donovan Jones."

"You found him," he retorted. "But I'm in a hell of a rush. I've got an appointment across town in fifteen minutes, and I'm going to be late as it is. Leave your name and number," he said, pushing a steno pad across the desk to him, "and I'll call you the first chance I get."

"No," the man said in the clipped regal way that only the British could do. "I need your help now."

Donovan wasn't a man who men often said no to. Straightening, he studied the hard look of determination in his visitor's eyes and the set of his jaw and recognized desperation when he saw it. "What's your story?" he demanded.

"I'm Buck Wyatt," he said. "I need you to find my sister."

Surprised, Donovan blinked. "I'm a bounty hunter, Mr. Wyatt. Is there a bounty out on your sister?"

"No. She's been kidnapped."

"How do you know that? Have you received a ransom demand?"

His mouth compressed in a flat line. "No. There won't be any ransom note. I already know what the kidnappers want."

Donovan knew he shouldn't have asked. He hadn't been lying about his meeting. He was going to be late, and it was important, dammit! But there was something in the fury in Buck Wyatt's eyes, something in the cold, controlled outrage in his voice that Donovan knew he wasn't going to be able to walk away from.

Resigned—and more than a little annoyed with his own curiosity—he motioned for Wyatt to pull up a chair. "You've got ten minutes," he said. "Make it good, because after that I am going to my meeting."

He didn't have to tell him twice. Too restless to take a seat, Buck Wyatt stood, instead...and paced. "My three sisters and I inherited a ranch in Colorado eleven months ago from an American cousin we didn't know we had," he said stiffly. "One of the stipulations of her will was that one of us had to be at the ranch at all times for a period of one year. There was no restriction on how many single nights we could be absent from the ranch, but if no member of the family is present for two nights running, the ranch goes to an unnamed heir."

Donovan lifted a brow at that. "How many people know about that little stipulation?"

"I would imagine just about everyone in the state of Colorado."

Donovan whistled softly. "And no one's run you off yet? You and your sisters must be damn tough."

A muscle clenched in Buck's jaw. "So far, we've managed to weather one attack after another...as long as they were against the ranch. Now they've gone after Priscilla a continent away."

"And you're sure your sister's kidnapping is related to the ranch? When's the year up?"

"Next month."

Donovan frowned. That changed things. "Are you even sure that she's really been kidnapped? What's her history? Is she the type to stage this kind of thing?"

"God, no! She's the baby of the family and damn stubborn sometimes about getting her way," he admitted honestly, "which is why she's in London to begin with. When she insisted on coming back to close up her apartment, we talked about her accident and how she could be walking right back into the same kind of danger as before, but she intended to be back in Colorado before anyone even knew she was gone. Obviously, that didn't happen."

"Whoa, back up," Donovan said sharply. "What accident?"

Buck quickly told him about the hit-and-run driver who'd nearly killed her. "She spent the last two months at the ranch, recuperating, and during that time, there wasn't a single attack against any of us because we were all together. Then, less than six hours after she arrives in London, someone grabs her."

"But how do you know that for sure? Maybe she just decided to go visit some friends before she left."

"She knew how important it was to get in and out as quickly as possible," Buck argued. "According to the London police, her landlord found the door to her flat standing wide-open and she was nowhere to be found. She appeared to be packing when someone apparently talked their way into her apartment. There were signs of a struggle and she left her purse behind."

Studying him through narrowed eyes, Donovan should have told him he couldn't help him. It would have been the wise thing to do. He was up to his ears in cases and couldn't even find the time to hire a decent secretary. He didn't have room on his calendar for another case.

And even if he had, he silently acknowledged, Priscilla Wyatt was not the kind of woman he wanted to go looking for. He'd read between the lines of what her brother had said about her, and she was obviously headstrong and spoiled and determined to have her way. Kidnapping her back from her kidnappers sounded like a headache waiting to happen.

But she was a woman in trouble. And unless he totally missed the mark, Buck was right. Her kidnapper was, no doubt, planning to use her as the pawn that drew her family away from the ranch. He would hurt her if he had to. Time was running out on the Wyatts's trial period, and whoever thought they were the unnamed heir had to be getting desperate. Priscilla Wyatt was in a hell of a mess…and in more danger than her family probably realized.

Silently swearing, Donovan pulled out his cell phone. Surprised, Buck Wyatt frowned. "What are you doing?"

"Canceling my appointment," he retorted. "I'll take the case."

Over the course of the next hour, Donovan asked Buck every question he could think of about Priscilla, her flat, where she might go if she was able to escape her kidnappers, how gutsy she was, her strengths and weaknesses. She'd been kidnapped. Would she fight or dissolve in tears? Panic or use her head? If he was going to save her, he had to know how she would react under duress.

"She'll use her head," Buck assured him. "Initially, she'll be scared out of her mind, but once she gets her fear under control, she'll start looking for a way to escape. She's smart," he added, "and damn creative. She won't take this lying down."

"That'll work in her favor as long as she doesn't let her kidnapper know what's going on in her head," Donovan replied. "The more helpless she acts, the better chance she'll have of taking the bastard by surprise. Has she ever taken any karate or self-defense classes?"

"No, not that I—"

His cell phone rang then, surprising them both.

Scowling at the number on the face of the phone, he looked up sharply at Donovan. "It's a private number."

"It could be the kidnapper," Donovan warned. "Don't let him know you're in London. And listen to background noises that might give you an indication of where he may be."

His expression grave, Buck nodded, then flipped open his phone. "Hello?"

"You have forty-eight hours to leave the ranch for good...or your sister dies."

"Who is this—"

Just that quickly, the line went dead. "He hung up," Buck said in disgust, and repeated word for word what the caller had said. "There weren't any background noises, and the bastard was definitely disguising his voice."

"Give me your cell phone number," Donovan told him. "I've got a friend who might be able to trace the caller's location when he made the call. I'll get back with you as soon as I know something."

"I'm going with you."

"The hell you are."

"Priscilla is my sister, dammit! I have a right—"

"Then find yourself another bounty hunter," he said curtly. "I work alone. If you really want to help your sister, go back to Colorado and help protect the rest of the family and your ranch. I'll take care of Priscilla."

"If she's still alive."

"Oh, she's alive," Donovan assured him. "She's got forty-eight hours. After that, all bets are off."

Chapter 2

The police had already gone through Priscilla's flat with a fine-tooth comb and released the place back to her landlord. Thanks to a call from Buck Wyatt, Donovan was able to get a spare key. He took one step inside and knew that at least two people were involved in her kidnapping.

And they hadn't taken her without a struggle.

Staring at the broken lamp and an overturned dining room chair, Donovan clenched his teeth on the sudden angry curse that rose to his tongue. Bastards. He didn't know Priscilla, didn't know any more about her than her brother had told him, but he knew all he needed to know. She might be spoiled and headstrong, but she was still an innocent woman who'd done nothing wrong except inherit a ranch from a distant relative she'd never met. She had, no doubt, been terrified when she realized that she'd opened her door to an enemy, but the lady had put up a fight. And it was that gumption that just might save her life.

The clock was ticking, and every instinct Donovan had urged him to hurry. Forty-eight hours would pass in the blink of an eye, and he was wasting precious time. But he knew from past cases that success depended on doing his homework. If he was going to find Priscilla Wyatt, he had to first know how her kidnappers had gotten her out of the apartment without someone noticing.

Walking over to the window that overlooked the street below, he frowned. The neighborhood that Priscilla lived in was in an older section of London that was a mix of well-known restaurants, popular pubs and shops at street level, with old-fashioned flats above. Considering that, Donovan doubted that the streets emptied before midnight. Which meant, he thought grimly, that Priscilla's kidnappers hadn't walked out of her flat with her like they were going out to dinner. So how the hell had they managed to get her out of her flat without anyone seeing them?

He turned to study the living room again, and only just then noticed what looked like a line of fine powder on the floor. Puzzled, he squatted down to examine it and realized that the powder was actually shattered glass from the lamp. And the reason it was in a neat line was because when the lamp broke, it had, apparently, shattered at the edge of a rug. A rug which was, he thought in growing fury, no longer there.

They'd rolled her up in a damn rug and carried her out like a dead body. He didn't care how gutsy she was; she must have been scared out of her mind.

Livid, he promised himself he was going to make the bastards pay for this. But first he had to find them.

His lean face carved in stern lines, he exited the apartment and made sure he locked the dead bolt. Then he went to work.

The neighborhood was quaint and full of atmosphere. The kind of place women loved, Donovan acknowledged...and a bitch to search. With the restaurants and pubs open late, people came and went at all hours of the day and night. God knew how many of them lived in the area or witnessed Priscilla's kidnapping without even knowing it.

Muttering a curse, he headed for the pub across the street. The bar had wide, paned windows that overlooked the street and Priscilla's flat. Surely a waitress or bartender or one of the regulars must have seen something.

But when he went inside, he was met with nothing but one negative response after another. Frustrated, he moved to the restaurant next door, then the bookstore on the corner and every other business up and down both sides of the street for three blocks. And the answer was always the same. No one had seen two men or anyone else moving a rug.

Walking out of the pizzeria two doors down from Priscilla's flat, he swore softly as he realized that darkness had fallen while he was canvassing the street and he still didn't have any leads to go on. And time was running out for Priscilla Wyatt.

It wasn't often that he was at his wit's end, and it infuriated him. He was better than this! His competitors claimed he had the nose of a bloodhound. So who the hell had taken Priscilla Wyatt?

Scowling, he stared down the street and watched the crowded sidewalks begin to empty as friends met friends for drinks or dinner and disappeared inside. The twilight was deeper now, the darkness nearly complete, and he realized that this was just about the time Priscilla must have been kidnapped. No wonder no one had noticed her kidnapping. The only street-lights were on the distant corners, and the people who were on the street were hurrying to get where they were going, not paying attention to anything but their own business.

Caught up in his musings, it was several long moments before he noticed the woman coming toward him, walking her dog. He started to look past her, only to glance at her sharply. Had she come by at the same time yesterday? People generally walked their dogs at the same time every day, didn't they? Could she have seen Priscilla's kidnappers in the dark and not even realized it? If she walked by without anyone else seeing her, the police wouldn't have questioned her because they had no idea she existed. Even now, twenty-four hours later, the woman probably didn't know that a kidnapping had taken place.

Striding toward her, he eyed her dog warily. A Doberman. Great, he thought irritably. He was usually good with dogs, but Dobermans could be damn pro-tective. The last one he'd tangled with had taken a bite out of his hide. He wasn't going there again.

"Nice dog," he told the woman as he drew closer. "Does he bite?"

"When I tell him to," she shot back. Stopping in her tracks, she tightened her grip on the leash. Just that easily, the dog was on guard. His golden brown eyes focused unblinkingly on Donovan, he growled low in his throat, daring him to take so much as one more step toward him and his mistress.

"Look, I'm not a threat to you," he told the woman. "I just need to ask you some questions. A woman was kidnapped here last night, and her family has hired me to find her."

"I didn't hear anything about a kidnapping," she replied, eyeing him suspiciously.

"The police didn't learn about it until late last night, and it didn't make the news until this morning," he explained.

Studying him, she frowned. "I was running late this morning," she finally admitted. "I haven't heard the news all day."

"Did you, by any chance, happen to walk this way last night?"

She didn't commit one way or the other. Instead, she just lifted a brow and said, "And if I did?"

"I'm not accusing you of anything," he assured her. "I just need to know if you saw two men moving a rug out of the flat across the street."

She didn't say a word, but even in the darkness, he saw surprise flicker in her eyes. "So you did see something," he said in satisfaction. "How many men were there? Two? Three? Did you get a look at them? What were they driving?" When she hesitated, he knew she didn't want to get involved. It was too late for that. "There was a woman rolled up in that rug," he said. "If the circumstances had been different, it could have been you. Are you really going to stand there and say nothing?"

For a moment, he thought she actually wasn't going to answer him. Then tears misted her eyes. "I didn't realize," she whispered, horrified. "It just looked like a rolled up rug—"

"She's still alive," he told her quietly. "But only for forty-eight hours."

"There were two men, both just a little taller than me. I didn't get a good look at their faces, but they were both very thin, almost gaunt."

"And their hair?"

"One was bald. And the other had a military cut. I think it was blonde."

Donovan frowned. *Military?* That was a twist he hadn't expected. "What were they driving?"

"A black van," she answered promptly. "I didn't get the plate number, but they didn't go very far. Just over to Reynolds Street."

Already trying to figure out how he was going to find two skinny, short bastards in a wrecked van, it was several seconds before her words registered. "What?" he said sharply. "How do you know that?"

"Because I saw the same van pulling out of an alley at Reynolds and Third when Precious and I were on our way home. Or at least I thought it was the same van," she added. "The streetlight on the corner was out, so I couldn't see very well."

"Reynolds and Third? You're sure?"

"Absolutely," she said. "C'mon. I'll show you. Though I don't know what good it will do. The van pulled out of the alley and disappeared down the street."

"That's okay," he replied. "It's a place to start. Let's go."

* * *

Ten minutes later, they reached Reynolds and Third. "The van came out of that alley," she said quietly, nodding toward the dark, narrow alley that disappeared between two buildings halfway down the street.

Studying the shadowy entrance to the alley, Donovan frowned. For the moment, he wasn't concerned with where the van had gone. Instead, he found it curious that Priscilla Wyatt's kidnappers had been in the alley to begin with. They hadn't, in all likelihood, driven into the alley by chance. So what the devil had they gone in there for?

His mind jumping with several interesting possibilities, he said, 'I'll check it out. Thanks for your help."

Tightening her grip on the Doberman's leash, his companion grimaced. "I didn't do much. I hope it helps."

Wishing him good-night, she and Precious continued their walk, but as Donovan strolled down the street to the entrance to the alley and peered in, his attention was on the upstairs apartments that overlooked the dark, narrow cavern. There was only one window lit, and a ragged curtain was doing its best to block the faint glimmer he saw in the darkness. What was up there?

Later, Donovan lost track of how long he stood deep in the shadows, watching, waiting for some sign that Priscilla Wyatt was in the apartment halfway down the alley. He knew there was a good possibility that he was wasting precious time while the kidnappers spirited Priscilla farther and farther from London. With every passing second, the trail that led to her whereabouts could be growing colder. But he didn't think so.

Something didn't smell right, and it wasn't just the rotting garbage in the trash can ten steps away from where he stood in the alley. It was the setup, he decided. The whole damn setup stank.

Lost in his musings, he almost didn't see the movement of the ragged curtain shrouding the lit window. Then he saw a man peer out into the darkness…a man with a military haircut.

Bingo.

An hour later, Donovan parked in the dark alley and soundlessly shut the driver's door of the small van he'd rented. Upstairs, there was no sign of the man he'd seen earlier, but the light was still on. If luck was with him—and he was feeling damn lucky!—Priscilla Wyatt was upstairs, waiting to be rescued, and her rescuers didn't have a clue their bird was about to fly the coop with a little help from him. There was nothing he liked better than surprises, he thought with a grin.

Checking to make sure his pistol was loaded, he quietly slipped into the building stairwell after picking the lock to the steel door that opened onto the alley. Standing in the darkness, he waited for his eyes to adjust to the deep shadows that engulfed him. From upstairs, the muffled sound of voices drifted down to him, but none of them were feminine. Donovan was far too good a tracker to be sidelined by that. Her kidnappers might be feeling pretty cocky right now, but unless they were complete novices, they weren't going to take any chances with her. Twenty-four hours after her kidnapping, they would still be watching her like a hawk so she couldn't give them away.

The question now, he thought pensively as he started up the stairs in the dark, was...how the hell was he going to get her out of the flat without getting them both killed? Her captors would be armed and had the advantage of knowing the layout of the flat. He didn't even know if Priscilla was bound, if he would have to carry her, if she would get hysterical when the bullets started flying. And there was no way to know until he burst through the door.

He was taking a hell of a risk, he silently acknowledged...and grinned wickedly at the thought. He'd always been a daredevil, which was what made him damn good at his job. If Priscilla Wyatt's kidnappers thought they had pulled a fast one on the authorities and the Wyatts, they were in for a rude awakening. They were toast. They just didn't know it yet.

Priscilla had never been so terrified in her life. The two thugs who had kidnapped her had removed the duct tape from her wrists and ankles, but they had other ways of keeping her captive. They'd made it clear that if she even moved toward the door or made so much as a sound, they would have one of her sisters or her brother killed.

And they could do it, she thought. They were ruthless—and in touch with someone in the States who was furious that her kidnapping hadn't drawn the rest of the family away from the ranch to London, as planned. Her captors informed her that the orders they were given were crystal clear—her siblings would be burying her if they didn't leave the ranch within forty-eight hours.

Her blood turning cold at the thought, she knew she had to get out of there. But her captors were in constant touch with their boss in the States. If she tried to escape, one of her siblings could be dead within the hour. How could she live with that on her conscience?

Suddenly furious, she decided right then and there that she wasn't going to take their abuse anymore. She was in charge of her own destiny, and she wasn't going to sit around on her hands and wait to die or let the bastards kill her family. She had to trust that Buck and her two future brothers-in-law, John and Hunter, would do everything they could to protect her sisters. In the meantime, she had to take care of herself.

Which meant, she decided resolutely, that she would kill her captors if she had to in order to keep herself and her family safe. The question was…how was she going to put them out of commission when they watched her like a hawk?

Lost in her musings, she didn't notice her captors whispering among themselves until one of them asked, "Are you hungry?"

It was a simple question, but she only eyed them suspiciously. Of course she was hungry! She hadn't had anything to eat since breakfast, when one of the men had left and returned a short while later with some pastries and a small bag of groceries. She'd been warned then that the pastries would be the only meal of the day. Leaving the flat was too risky, so the groceries they'd bought would be saved for tomorrow. So why were they asking her now if she was hungry? What kind of game were they playing? If they thought they were going to surprise her into saying something so they would have a reason to kill Katherine or Elizabeth or Buck, they were wasting their time. She wasn't saying a word.

"Who cares if she's hungry or not," the other kidnapper snapped. "My stomach feels like my throat's been cut, and I'm not waiting until tomorrow to eat." Sneering at Priscilla, he said, "Cook us something to eat, bitch. And don't even think about trying anything fishy. We've already got orders to kill you tomorrow. We'd just as soon do it now as then, so don't push your luck."

Nodding silently, she kept her eyes down as she headed for the kitchen so he wouldn't see the anger she knew was reflected there. If she acted meek and afraid, maybe they would drop their guard and relax enough for her to put something in their food. Surely there had to be some kind of pesticide or drain cleaner under the sink. *Something…*

Her eyes suddenly landed on the prescription bottle that one of her captors had set on the windowsill above the kitchen sink. She'd seen him take a couple of pills right after breakfast. What was he taking? Was it something that she could drug both men with?

Fighting the urge to hurry to the sink to check out the prescription, she reminded herself that her every move was being watched. So she headed for the refrigerator, instead, for the groceries that *Baldy* had deposited there, bag and all, that morning after he'd gone shopping.

Her heart pounding, she set the groceries on the kitchen counter and cast a quick glance at the prescription bottle that was less than three feet away. She only saw two words before she turned her attention back to the food, but it was enough. *Blood pressure.*

Elated, she almost laughed out loud. Yes! If she gave them enough, it would lower their blood pressure and knock them out, wouldn't it? She could mix it with…*roast beef*?! Swallowing a groan, she blinked back tears. What was she supposed to do with canned roast beef and potatoes? At least there was tea, too. She could make it extra strong, then lace it liberally with the medication. It wasn't much of a plan, but it was the only one she had. First, however, she had to get her hands on the medication without anyone noticing.

The opportunity came much quicker than she'd anticipated. She'd just found a saucepan and a can opener when what sounded like a shot exploded on the dark street down below.

"What the hell!" her bald captor swore and ran to the bedroom to check the view from there.

"What is it?" the other man yelled to his partner as he took up a position at the living room window. "Was that a shot? I can't see anything for the fog."

Taking advantage of the distraction, Priscilla grabbed the prescription bottle, popped the lid and sent up a silent prayer of thanks when she saw the bottle was nearly full. Hurriedly pouring pills into her hand, she pocketed them, capped the bottle and returned it to the windowsill in four seconds flat.

"I think a car backfired," Baldy said in disgust. "It must have been amplified by the fog."

Afraid to look over her shoulder to see if either one of the men had seen her, she tried to act as casual as possible when she found a can opener and opened the roast beef; but it wasn't easy. Her heart was slamming against her ribs, her fingers were trembling and she was sure they only had to look into her eyes to know that she was up to something. She needn't have worried, however. Her captors were too concerned with what was going on downstairs on the street to pay any attention to her.

Then, with no warning, there was a knock at the door.

Priscilla whirled to face her captor by the living room window, only to find him glaring at her like she was somehow responsible for the knock at the door. Pale, she took a step back. His expression furious, he made a sharp silencing motion, then strode over to the door.

The visitor knocked again, this time louder. "Mr. Smith? Are you in there?"

"You've got the wrong address," Baldy growled through the closed door. "Go away."

If the man on the other side of the door heard him, he gave no sign of it. Instead, he knocked loudly on the door again and shouted, "Mr. Smith? I've got a package for you. The postman delivered it to my place by mistake this afternoon."

"I told you you've got the wrong place! Get the hell away from my door or—"

He never had a chance to finish the threat. A split second later, the door was kicked open and he found himself confronting a tall man with a ski mask pulled down over his face. Before Baldy could even think to yell for his partner for help, he was shocked with a stun gun and went down.

Donovan stepped over the man and took in the rest of the flat in a single, all-encompassing glance. Priscilla was in the kitchen and was pale as a ghost as her eyes met his. He didn't have time to reassure her—not when the second kidnapper was already charging toward him, reaching for his gun. Donovan had two seconds, at the most. Rushing him before he could pull his gun completely free, Donovan hit him with the stun gun and sent him to the floor.

There was, after that, no time to waste. Lightning quick, he handcuffed first one man, then the other. Then he slapped duct tape over their mouths and tied their feet together. That would hold them long enough for him to get Priscilla out of London, where he could keep her safe until he was able to hand her over to her brother.

But when he turned to grab her and hustle her out of the apartment, she was gone and the door to the flat was standing wide open.

"Son of a bitch!"

Running after her, he practically threw himself down the stairs, taking them two at a time in the darkness and nearly breaking his neck in the process. He couldn't lose her, dammit! If she disappeared into the streets of London at this time of night, he'd have a devil of a time picking up her trail again.

The second he took the last step, he hit the steel door that opened onto the alley and burst outside, only to stop in his tracks as fog slapped him right in the face. "What the—"

The fog had slipped in like a thief in the night while he was waiting in the stairwell, sliding down alleys and streets and into darkened doorways, and with no effort whatsoever, he could imagine himself in Victorian London, when Jack the Ripper walked the streets. Visibility was down to fifty feet, and if Priscilla Wyatt was out there somewhere, there was no sign of her.

When he got his hands on her, he was going to give her a piece of his mind. But first he had to find her, and his task had just become nearly impossible. Where the hell could she have gone? The van he'd rented blocked one end of the alley, but squeezing past it would have slowed her down. Making a snap decision, he turned and ran in the opposite direction.

Sounds carried in the fog, and as he reached the cross street at the end of the alley, a car screeched to a stop half a block away. He turned sharply...just in time to see someone dart right in front of an oncoming car that suddenly seemed to appear out of nowhere. In the watery light of the vehicle's headlights, he caught just a glimpse of a woman running like the hounds of hell were after her. Almost immediately, she was swallowed by the fog again, but not before he recognized Priscilla Wyatt.

"Dammit, where is she going?" he said as he tore off his mask and took off after her.

Darting across the street, he just barely missed being flattened by a taxi. The taxi driver swore at him and laid on his horn, but he didn't spare the man a glance. Instead, his eyes were locked on the spot where Priscilla had disappeared into the thickening fog. There was a streetlight on the corner and then nothing but darkness for at least two blocks. He only had seconds to catch her or he'd be chasing shadows in the dark.

Suddenly, the fog shifted eerily in front of him like a living thing. For the span of a heartbeat, Priscilla was just three steps in front of him. That was all he needed to grab her.

The hand that came out of the darkness to snare her

wrist stopped Priscilla's heart in mid beat. Terrified, she screamed even as she turned on her kidnapper like a woman possessed. "Let go of me, you bastard! My husband will kill you!"

"I'm not going to hurt you!" her attacker growled. "Shut up before you get us both killed!"

Shut up? He was kidnapping her and he expected her to *shut up*?! The hell she would! Digging in her heels, moaning as his fingers threatened to crush the bones in her wrist as he jerked her toward him, she screamed, "Help! Somebody help me! I'm being kidnapped!"

Chapter 3

Across the street, a woman who was just getting out of a taxi stepped onto the curb, only to freeze at Priscilla's cry. Frowning in their direction, she tried to see them in the shifting fog. "Who's there?" she called. "Are you all right?"

"Help me! I'm being kidnapped!"

"No, she's not," Donovan called out quickly as he hauled her close and clamped his hand over her mouth. "She's a thief!"

Outraged, she bit him…and regained the freedom of speech when he swore and jerked his hand free. "I am not! Let go of me, you bastard!"

"Not on your life, sweetheart," he said, fighting to control her. Damn, she was strong! And quick. She kicked him before he even guessed her intentions, then somehow managed to evade his efforts to haul her

against him and stifle her cries. "She stole a pair of
diamond earrings from Thompson's Jewelry Store,"
Donovan told the woman. "I'm an undercover security
officer for the store. I saw her take the earrings and
stroll out without batting an eye. And they were five
hundred pounds!"

He came up with the story on the spot, and it was a
damn good one. Thompson's Jewelry Store was two
blocks over, not far from Priscilla's flat, and the
woman Priscilla was appealing to for help obviously
knew that. She bought the story lock, stock and barrel.
"I've got no use for thieves," she retorted coldly. "Haul
her ass off to jail. She deserves it."

Outraged, Priscilla tried to protest, but all she could
manage was a muffled cry as Donovan started to drag
her away into the fog…and darkness. "C'mon," he
said roughly, "you're going to show me where you
ditched the earrings, then you're going to have a nice
long chat with the police."

Helpless, overpowered, but still struggling, Priscilla couldn't believe this was happening. She'd
escaped her kidnappers, only to fall into the hands of
another one? No! Somebody had to help her. There
were still people out on the street, cars passing by.
Surely someone would step forward…

But no one did. The fog swallowed them whole, and
just that quickly, she was alone with a stranger who
suddenly dragged her into an alley…the same one
she'd run down when she'd escaped from her kidnappers. Was he taking her back? Or did he have more
sinister plans for her? The alley was pitch black,

deserted. And he could do anything he wanted to her…hurt her…rape her…kill her.

Panic pooled in her mouth at the thought. No! She couldn't just go meekly along with him. If he thought he would overpower her without a fight, he was in for a rude awakening. She'd gouge his eyes out—

"I'm not going to hurt you," he growled in a low whisper that didn't carry past her ears. "Your brother sent me."

If he hadn't had his hand clamped over her mouth, she would have laughed. *Her brother?!* Yeah, right. Did he really think she was stupid enough to buy that story? The only way he could know she had a brother was if he was hired by the same man who sent the first set of kidnappers after her. The same man, she thought, blanching, who'd ordered her to be killed if her family didn't leave the ranch in forty-eight hours.

Clawing at the hand that pinched her mouth to keep her quiet, she knew her new kidnapper wasn't going to wait forty-eight hours. He was going to kill her now and get it over with.

Terrified, she kicked and clawed and silently called him every filthy name she could think of. For a moment, she thought she was making progress when the heel of her hand connected with his nose. He grunted…and locked his fingers around her wrists like a set of hand-cuffs. In the next instant, he jerked her hands behind her, and before she could do anything but gasp, she was chest to chest with him and totally helpless.

Caught in the trap of his steely blue gaze, she froze…and heard the roar of her blood in her ears. Suddenly, she was aware of just how strong he was, how close, how hard. Her mouth went dry, and she should have been scared out of her mind. Instead, she'd never been so furious in her life. How dare he manhandle her! "Let go of me, you slimy piece of—"

In the darkness, his eyes narrowed, but he only snapped, "Watch your mouth. I'm trying to help you, but if you insist on doing this the hard way, you'll be the one who suffers." And with no more warning than that, he jerked open the driver's door of the van she'd seen in the alley earlier and pushed her inside.

He released her for just a second so he could climb in after her, but that was all the time she needed. Sobbing, she threw herself across the van and jerked open the passenger door.

Run. Run. RUN! a voice screamed in her ear, but her feet never had a chance to hit the pavement. An arm snaked around her waist, snaring her, and she was hauled, kick and screaming, back into the van and tossed into her seat like a sack of potatoes.

"Bastard! Jerk! You're not going to get away with this! Do you hear me? My brother will hunt you down like the miserable scumbag you are and make you wish you'd never laid eyes on me. *Let go of me!*"

"No problem," he snarled, and hit the door lock, making it impossible for her to escape. She was still cussing at him when he jerked out his phone and punched in a number. When the caller came on the line, he held the phone out to her. "It's your brother," he told her coldly.

Stunned, she grabbed the phone. "Buck?"

"Are you all right?"

Tears welled in her eyes at the sound of her brother's familiar voice. "I thought I was being kidnapped again."

"You were," he said gruffly. "It was the only way I could think of to get you back. Did they hurt you?"

They both knew he was asking if she'd been raped. "No," she choked. "They were more interested in killing me in forty-eight hours."

"I knew the minute I met Donovan, he'd find you. He's a bounty hunter," he added. "You're in good hands, Sis."

"I'm sorry I insisted on coming back," she said tearfully. "How did anyone know I was here?"

"I don't know—I'm still trying to figure that out. For now, though, you're safe," he assured her. "That's what's important. Now we just have to keep you that way. Let me talk to Donovan again."

"You mean the Neanderthal?"

He chuckled. "Be nice. He's your new best friend."

"Yeah, right," she sniffed, and handed the phone to the man who was grinning at her smugly. "Buck wants to talk to you."

Taking the phone, he said, "Yes, sir?"

"I owe you."

"No, you don't," Donovan said easily. "I was just doing my job. So what's next? Where are you? I'll drop her off wherever you're staying."

"I appreciate the offer," Buck said, "but plans have changed. I need you to keep her with you for the next month."

Donovan nearly dropped the phone. "You must be joking."

"It's the only way to keep her safe."

"The hell it is!" he retorted. "She'll be a hell of a lot safer in Colorado. She can be back with her family at the ranch by this time tomorrow."

"She'll never get that far," Buck said soberly. "They know she couldn't have gone far. Whoever arranged this is probably already turning the city upside down looking for her. She's in danger until the ranch is ours. She needs you. *We* need you."

Donovan didn't doubt for a second that he could protect her, but was he prepared to spend a month with her? The lady was a handful—and she didn't trust him as far as she could throw him. If he was dumb enough to do this, he knew she'd make his life a living hell.

"No," he said firmly. "I'm not a babysitter. That wasn't part of the deal."

"You'll be doing a hell of a lot more than babysitting," Buck told him. "I don't have time to go into everything right now—my flight back to the States has just been called—but the bastards who kidnapped her are bound to be watching the airports, hoping to get their hands on her a second time. And if they do, they'll kill her this time. That's how badly they want the ranch."

"Which is why you need to get her out of the country as soon as possible," Donovan pointed out.

"I realize that, but it's not that easy, dammit. I've dealt with this for nearly a year, and it's like trying to catch a ghost. We don't know what the enemy looks like. It could be anyone, including the baggage clerk at the airport, which means Priscilla's not safe anywhere...except with you." He exhaled. "You're damn resourceful—you found her when no one else could. You'll be able to keep her safe until you can find a way to get her out of England. I don't know anyone else who can do that."

At a loss, Donovan hesitated. Did Buck know what he was asking of him? "I don't know, Buck..."

"I'll double your fee."

Donovan liked to think he wasn't a fool, especially when it came to money. A job was a job. And he could handle little Miss Priss. "All right," he said. "But you can tell her. She's not going to be happy about it."

"I can't," he said. "We're about to take off—we've just been told to turn off all electronics. Tell Priscilla I love her and I'll see her in a month. Keep her safe. I'm counting on you."

"Wait a minute. What if—" That was as far as he got before the line went dead. Swearing, Donovan snapped the phone shut and tossed it into a cupholder. "Great! This is just great!"

Beside him, Priscilla eyed him suspiciously. "What is? What am I not going to be happy about? What did Buck say?"

"He's pretty sure the airports are being watched," he said bluntly, "so leaving the country, at least for now, is out of the question. He thinks you'll be safer with me, anyway."

"*What?!* Oh, no. I'm going home."

"Not right now you're not," he informed her. "He just hired me to watch over you for the next month."

"The hell he did!"

A grin propped up one side of his mouth. So the fireworks were about to begin. "He doubled my fee, sweetheart," he chuckled. "Like it or not, it looks like you're stuck with me."

"For a *month?* You're out of your mind. In case you hadn't noticed, I'm not a child."

Appreciation glinted in his eyes. "Oh, I noticed, all right."

She gave him a withering look. "Stuff it, Mr.—" Trying to remember his name, she frowned. "What the devil *is* your name? Dirk? Darryl?"

"Donovan Jones," he said with a grin. "But you can call me Mr. Jones."

"In your dreams," she snorted. "Keep this up and I'll call you—"

"Wonderful…studly…Superman—"

"Irritating…obnoxious—"

"George."

Surprised, she blinked. "George?"

"Clooney."

Caught off guard, she laughed. "You must be joking."

For a moment, she thought she'd insulted him. Something that looked like hurt flashed in his steely blue eyes. Then she saw his lips twitch, and alarm bells went off in her head. He was, she realized, far more dangerous than she'd first suspected. He was one of those men who was far too sure of himself, who knew how to set a woman's heart pounding with just a smile and a twinkle in his eyes. And she had to spend a month with him? No way!

"I'm calling Buck," she told him, snatching up his phone. "I don't need anyone to take care of me."

"You'd have a better argument if I hadn't just rescued you from those two thugs," he pointed out dryly, "but go ahead and call him. It's not going to do you any good. He's already on a plane back to the States."

She didn't believe him. Lightning quick, she punched in Buck's cell phone, but it never rang. Instead, it went straight to voice mail. Swearing, she hung up. "How much is he paying you?" she demanded. "Whatever it is, I'll double it."

He grinned. "Really? What is it with you people? First your brother, now you. You do realize, don't you, that you're quadrupling my original fee without even knowing what it is?"

"It doesn't matter," she snapped. "I'll come up with the money someway. Are you accepting my offer or not?"

"It depends on what you want me to do," he said simply.

"Take me to Heathrow."

"Forget it!" he said quickly. "That's out of the question."

"Then take me to Bristol or Liverpool."

"Nope. It's too dangerous."

"You don't know that."

"The hell I don't. Buck told me all about the problems your family is having in Colorado. Someone wants the ranch, sweetheart, and it sounds like they're willing to commit murder to get it. In case you missed who their intended victim is, it's you."

A cold shiver skated down her spine. Hugging herself, she stared out the van's passenger window as they raced across London in the fog at a frightening speed. "Oh, no," she said huskily. "I knew. I was hoping they were just trying to scare me."

"Did it work?"

Her throat dry, she nodded. "That's why I ran when you broke in. I knew it was the only chance I was going to get."

"And you still want me to take you to the airport? Are you crazy, girl? Buck was right—they'll be watching the airports. You'd be running right into a trap."

"Not if we got there before they did," she pointed out. "They don't know where we're going—"

He laughed without humor. "Of course they know where we're going! It's the only way back to the States, sweetheart, unless you're going to take a slow boat to China."

"But we left them back at the flat. We've got a head start."

He couldn't believe she was serious. "Yes, we do, but how do you know the clowns I tied up back at the flat are the only ones after you? The bastard who sent them after you appears to have a hell of a long reach. Do you really think he wouldn't have a backup in place in case you were able to escape?"

Horrified, Priscilla felt her heart drop into her stomach. "You mean we're being followed? Oh, God! Where—"

He checked the rearview mirror for the tenth time in two minutes, but the fog that surrounded them was all encompassing. "Relax," he told her. "Nothing short of a bloodhound's following us in this fog. By the time it lifts, we'll have left London far behind. Not that anyone needs to follow us," he added. "All your kidnappers have to do is watch the airports...and the Paris tunnel. Those are the only two ways to get off this island, which is why we're avoiding them."

"Then where are we going?"

"I'm still working on that. Buck caught me off guard," he admitted. "But don't worry. I'll take care of everything."

After everything she'd been through, trust was no longer something she gave easily. Eyeing him warily in the dim glow of the dash lights, she lifted a delicately arched brow. "Really? I'm supposed to trust you, just like that? How do I know you're not working with my kidnappers and taking me back to them?"

"You talked to Buck," he reminded her. "He told you himself that he hired me."

"But how did he get your name? You're a bounty hunter. Why didn't he hire a private investigator instead? Who recommended you to him?"

He shrugged. "That's something you'll have to ask him."

"I can't. He's on a plane for the next ten hours."

Not the least disturbed, he said, "That's your problem, Miss Priss. Some things you just have to take on faith."

"No, I don't," she said sharply. "Not when my life is on the line.

"Your life won't be on the line as long as you do what I say," he reminded her. "So from now on, you don't ask questions, you don't hesitate, you don't argue. Understood?"

Lifting her chin, she gave him a cool look. "Not in a million years. I'm not one of the low-life criminals you make your living catching, so save your little speech for someone who needs a keeper. Believe it or not, I have a brain under all this strawberry-blond hair, and I don't need you to tell me I'm in danger. I was the one who was kidnapped, remember?"

"And the one who opened the door to your kidnapper," he reminded her mockingly. "So tell me again about the brain under all that blond hair."

"Go to hell."

He only grinned. "I've already been there and back, sweetheart. I'm not going anywhere without you."

Fuming, she was tempted to smack him, but she wasn't that kind of woman. "He told me he was a cop," she said stiffly. "He had a badge—"

"I can't believe you fell for that," he groaned, rolling his eyes. "That's one of the oldest tricks in the book. I've used it myself."

"Trust me—I won't make that mistake again. I felt like a fool."

"Good. There's hope for you yet. Don't trust anyone—I don't care what badge they're flashing or what story they tell you. As far as you're concerned, everyone you see and talk to is after you."

She lifted a delicately arched brow at him. "Including you?"

He grinned. "I don't go *after* the chicks in my custody. Afterward…" He shrugged. "Give me a call, sweetheart. We'll talk about it."

"In your dreams," she sniffed.

When she lifted her pert little nose in the air, Donovan laughed. So he wasn't good enough for her, huh? They'd see about that. The day would come when he would make the lady purr just to prove he could. But not now. Not when they were practically shackled and stuck with each other for the next month. For now, he had to come up with a plan to keep her safe.

His phone rang then, shattering the silence that had fallen between then. Looking at the caller ID, he swore. Tim Elliot. He was a snitch with a taste for scotch who knew more about what was going on in the back alleys of London than just about anyone Donovan knew. And he didn't call unless he had a lead he knew Donovan was willing to pay for.

His timing couldn't have been worse, but Donovan knew he couldn't afford to ignore the call. If Tim was in need of a drink, he'd go to the perp himself and give Donovan up without a thought for a bottle of scotch.

Snatching up the phone, he barked, "What?"

"I just had a drink with Leo Guardino."

Donovan clenched his teeth. Leo Guardino was one of the biggest prizes out there—wanted for murder and drug smuggling, he had a 20,000 quid price on his head. Rumors had floated around for the last year that he was dead, but Donovan knew better. There'd been times when he'd been so close to the bastard that he could smell him, but he'd always managed to disappear like smoke in the wind. How the devil had Tim found him?

"Where?"

"The Pirate's Cove."

Donovan knew the pub well. It was a dive on a dark, ancient street in the heart of London where no decent person would step foot. The patrons there dealt in drugs and weapons and every kind of contraband known to man, and few, if any of them, remembered what it was like to have a soul. Even the cops didn't go there if they could avoid it, and Donovan couldn't blame them. It was a sinister place.

"You didn't give me up, did you, Tim? You wouldn't do that to a friend, would you?"

"No. No! No way, man! You know me better than that. I work with you all the time. You can trust me."

Donovan could practically feel him sweating through the phone. *Trust him?* Not in a million years.

"I'm glad to hear it," he said coolly. "I would hate like hell to think you would betray me after everything I've been through with you. You know, like that incident at The Royal Arms, when you—"

"I'm with you, Donny boy. I'm your man. That's why I called. I wanted to let you know where Guardino was. Right now, he's living in a flat around the corner from the Pirate's Cove, but he's not staying there long. He said something about going down to Southampton."

Donovan swore. Southampton, where he could jump a ship and sail away to anywhere. And he was stuck babysitting little Miss Priss while 20,000 quid sailed away. Damn!

"I can't do anything about it now," he growled. "Maybe later. Keep me posted." Hanging up without another word, he raced around a Mercedes that pulled out in front of him, muttering curses all the while.

Her gaze trained straight ahead, Priscilla hung on for dear life. Who was this man? she wondered wildly. What had possessed her brother to hire him? What did he know about him? Was he really a bounty hunter…or as bad as the criminals he claimed to catch?

She mentally relayed the veiled threat he'd issued during his terse phone call. Who was Tim and what kind of crime had they committed together? Was he blackmailing him? It certainly sounded like he was holding something over his head, but what? What happened at The Royal Arms? Was there a fight…a robbery…a murder?

Alarmed by the direction of her thoughts, she told herself she was just letting her imagination run away with her. Buck wouldn't have hired a criminal to find her. He would have done some research.

But even as she tried to reassure herself she had nothing to worry about, she knew Buck hadn't had any time to check out anyone. He'd flown to London as soon as the police had notified him of her kidnapping. And considering how quickly Donovan had found her, Buck must have hired him almost immediately. When would he have had time to do a background check?

Her breath caught in her throat at the thought. How could she trust him? Even if he really was a bounty hunter, he hunted down people for money. His only loyalty was to whoever paid him. What if the devil who was after the ranch had discovered that Buck had hired him, then offered him more money to get rid of her? It would be so easy. All he had to do was pretend that he was taking her somewhere to protect her, then eliminate her when he was sure there was no one around to witness her murder. He could dump her body in the middle of nowhere. All he would have to tell Buck was that she'd gotten away from him, her kidnappers had caught her again, then dispose of her body. Just that easily, Donovan and the jackasses who had taken her captive would get away with murder, and no one would be the wiser.

The coppery taste of fear in her mouth sickening her, she was afraid in a way she hadn't been before. He wasn't like the kidnappers who'd forced their way into her apartment last night. They'd been cold and threatening and more than a little sinister, and she readily admitted that they'd terrified her, but she'd recognized fairly quickly that they weren't the brightest bulbs in the box. Donovan, on the other hand, was not the kind of man who suffered fools lightly. Sharp intelligence gleamed in his blue eyes, along with a steely determination that chilled her to the bone. When he smiled, he fairly oozed charm, but Priscilla knew better than to be taken in by the man's good looks and crooked grin. He was dangerous, and the quicker she got away from him the better.

He didn't make it easy for her. He drove long into the night, leaving the fog of London—and, hopefully, her kidnappers—far behind. Still, he refused to stop in spite of the fact that she'd had nothing to eat since breakfast and was feeling nauseated. It wasn't until she warned him that she was going to throw up if she didn't get something in her stomach that he finally stopped at the next petrol station they came to.

"This is the only stop we're making between now and dawn," he warned her as he took advantage of the stop to fill up the van with gas. Pulling out his wallet, he handed her some cash. "I suggest you get enough junk food to last you for the next twelve hours or so. Once the sun comes up, we'll hole up somewhere for the rest of the day. You can whine all you want—we're not leaving there until it's dark tomorrow night, so get what you want to eat now."

"Just because I'm hungry doesn't mean I'm a whiner. You'd be complaining too if you hadn't eaten in sixteen hours."

"You're a wuss," he retorted. "You're the baby of the family, aren't you?" When she just looked at him, he grinned. "I knew it. I bet your parents carried you around on a feather pillow and gave little Miss Priss everything she wanted, didn't they?"

He couldn't have been more wrong about her, but she had no intention of dignifying his accusations with an answer. Turning on her heel, she marched into the petrol station with her nose in the air.

"Do you want me to get the food for you, baby?" he called after her. "I can feed it to you, too, if you want."

Walking across the parking lot to the petrol station, she gave him a rude hand gesture, which only drew a laugh from him. Obnoxious man, she thought, fighting to hold back a smile. She would not laugh! He might be irritatingly charming, but for all she knew, he was just another kidnapper working for whoever was after the Broken Arrow. And she was getting away from him just as soon as possible.

Her chance came much quicker than she'd anticipated. When she walked into the petrol station and headed for the restroom, her breath caught in her throat at the sight of the alcove next to the restrooms that was the entrance to the station's storage room. A sign above the doorway said Employees Only, but she hardly noticed. All she saw was the rear door at the far end of the storage room. It was standing wide open for the deliveryman, who was wheeling in boxes of supplies. Without a word to him or anyone else, she walked past him, slipped outside and disappeared into the darkness behind the rear of the building.

Chapter 4

Later, Donovan would have sworn that Priscilla couldn't have been out of his sight for more than a minute or two. But when he went into the station to pay, she was nowhere to be found.

"Dammit to hell!" Swearing, he knocked sharply on the door to the women's restroom, but there was no response. When he glanced inside, the room was empty.

"I'm going to kill her," he muttered to himself, not bothering to ask the clerk where she'd gone. The answer was obvious. A deliveryman was busy restocking the snack aisle with fresh breads and cakes, and through the station's storage room, he could see the back door to the building. It was standing wide open.

Kicking himself for being seven kinds of a fool—and ever saying yes to Buck Wyatt—he ran out the door, promising himself he was going to hog-tie her when he got his hands on her again. Then he caught a glimpse of her—a dark shadow running down the street…just as a car came around the corner behind her. She never saw the driver speed up, never saw him send the vehicle racing right at her.

He was going to hit her.

Donovan wasn't a man who was easily shaken, but momentarily, he stood rooted to the ground. Then he started running. *"Priscilla!"*

Startled, she turned, and even in the dark, Donovan would have sworn she went white as a sheet when she saw the car shooting toward her like a bullet. She screamed and threw herself behind a tree. A split second later, the oncoming vehicle caught the edge of the tree, bounced off it and went careening across the street to slam into a Mini Cooper heading the opposite direction.

Donovan didn't wait to see more. Reaching Priscilla, he grabbed her. "C'mon!" he shouted. "We've got to get out of here. Now!"

He didn't have to tell her twice. Turning, she ran back to the van with him and threw herself inside like the devil himself was after her. The second Donovan slid behind the wheel, she hit the door locks.

"I ought to turn you over my knee," he snarled as he started the engine with a quick flick of his wrist and pulled out of the petrol station parking lot with squealing tires. "What the hell were you thinking? I told you you were safe with me. How many times do I have to say it? You even talked to Buck, for God's sake!"

Stung, she snapped, "Anyone can say anything. I heard what you said to that man who called you. You accused him of giving you up, of betraying you—"

"He's a snitch," he cut in. "He'd just had a pint with a bastard I'd been tracking for over a year! I was afraid he'd told him I was after him." Checking his rearview mirror, he took little comfort in the fact that there wasn't a soul behind them. "How the hell did they find us?" he muttered half to himself.

Seeing the direction of his gaze, she glanced sharply over her shoulder. "Are we being followed?"

"No," he retorted. "We weren't before."

Surprised, she frowned. "Then how—"

"That's what I'm trying to figure out. They couldn't have staked out our route—I didn't know where I was going until after I spoke to Buck. So how could they have known what direction we were going and already put thugs in place to intercept us?"

"Surely they don't have enough manpower to watch every road coming out of London," she said, confused. "That would take dozens of men."

"It would take a hell of a lot more than that," he said grimly. "And even then, they'd have to scour every road in London, which is, of course, impossible."

"Then how—"

"They've got to be tracking us." Swearing, he turned off the road abruptly and whipped behind a closed restaurant. Braking quickly, he threw the transmission into park and pushed open his door. "C'mon," he told her, "there's got to be a bug planted on the van somewhere. We've got to find it."

"A bug? But how—"

"Someone must have planted it when it was parked in the alley behind your flat."

"But how? When?" Then she remembered the threats

her captors had made just minutes before Donovan had burst into the apartment. "Oh, my God, my kidnappers were expecting someone," she told him as she slipped out of the van and joined him. "He was late, and they kept telling me he was going to torture me and record my screams for my family. If he came in after I escaped, he would have seen the van in the alley."

"And assumed whoever left it there had something to do with your escape."

"But he didn't know that for sure. So why didn't he come looking for us?"

"He did—that's why he wasn't at the van when we got back," he replied. "And he didn't have to be if he had it bugged. If he missed you in the fog, which he obviously did, all he had to do was track the van."

Horrified, she looked at the van like it was some kind of monster. "Where would he hide a bug? What does it look like?"

"Tracking devices come in different shapes, but it's small and it's magnetic. So look under the fenders and bumpers—any place you could stick a magnet where it might not be noticed."

The restaurant they'd parked behind was closed and pitch black. The parking lot had lights, but they, too, were dark, and the closest available streetlight was nearly three blocks away. With no flashlight, they were left with no choice but to blindly run their hands over the vehicle in search of the tracking device that could have been anywhere.

Priscilla had little experience with the nuts and bolts of a van or any other automobile, let alone a bug smaller than a walnut that could track them across

England. She couldn't find anything…or shake the feeling that they were being watched. Panic pulling at her, she glanced over her shoulder for the fifth time in less than a minute and had to fight the need to run. Was that eyes she saw in the darkness?

"We need to get out of here!" she finally cried. "We've been here too long. They're going to find us."

"Check the rear bumper one more time," he told her. "The damn thing's got to be here somewhere."

Frustrated, she did as he instructed, but only because he wouldn't agree to leave until she did. "This is crazy! You're going to get us killed—"

At that moment, her fingers whisked over a metal disc that she hadn't noticed before because she hadn't reached completely under the middle of the bumper. Her pulse racing, she reached deep again, blindly examining the unknown object with her fingertips, looking for an edge she could slip a nail under. When she found it, the small piece of metal dropped into her hand.

"Got it," she said, and held it up triumphantly.

"Good girl," he exclaimed, pleased, as he examined it. "Now that we know what we're dealing with, let's get the hell out of here."

She expected him to throw the tracking device into the middle of the nearest field. Instead, he took it with them. Horrified, she watched as he casually dropped it into a cup holder on the console between the two front seats. "What are you doing? I thought you were going to get rid of it. It's going to lead the kidnappers right to us!"

Far from worried, he only grinned in the darkness. "Ye of little faith. Chill, sweetheart. I've got everything under control."

If she hadn't been so worried, she would have laughed at the outrageous remark. *Under control?!* He was driving around with the bug that would lead her kidnappers right to them, and he wasn't the least bit concerned. Was he mad? How could she possibly chill when there were men chasing them, men who knew where they were and wanted her dead?

"That's easy for you to say," she began, only to frown when he suddenly did a U-turn in the middle of the road and pulled into a petrol station. "What are you doing? We already have petrol."

Pulling up next to the gas tank, where a truck loaded with restaurant supplies was also parked, he reached for the bug and shot her a quick grin. "Watch and learn."

Stepping from the van, he disappeared behind the restaurant supply truck. Anyone watching him would think that he was heading for the petrol station to prepay for his gas, but he was back almost immediately. And there was no sign of the tracking device.

Priscilla immediately guessed what he had done and she was aghast. "How could you put it on that truck? That poor driver is totally innocent in all this. What's he going to do when he's chased down by the kidnappers?"

"Tell them that the only time he stopped was to get gas," he said simply, "and he never saw anyone stick a bug on his truck. By the time they figure out where the switch was made, we'll be long gone."

"But what if they don't believe him?" she argued. "They could threaten him."

"And risk bringing the police in on this? I don't think so. Relax. You're safe," he assured her, and turned right as he pulled out of the station.

Surprised, she frowned at the sight of London in the distance. "What are you doing? We're going the wrong way. This takes us back to London!"

"I know," he confirmed. "We're going back to your flat."

"What?!"

"We don't have any choice," he explained. "Unless you have your passport with you..."

"My passport? Oh, my God!"

"Why don't I like the sound of that? What's wrong? Where's your passport?"

"The kidnappers threw it away so I wouldn't be able to leave the country if I managed to escape from them. Now what do we do?"

"Don't panic," he said quickly. "First things first. Are you sure they threw it away? Did you actually see them toss it?"

She nodded. "They threw it in the Dumpster in the alley. What if it's been emptied?"

"Then we'll deal with it," he replied. "If we have to, we can use a fake passport, but I don't want to risk that unless we're absolutely forced to—which is why we're going back to your flat."

Priscilla's stomach turned over at the thought. "Why can't we go to the police? Or Scotland Yard? If the authorities knew what was going on, surely they'd be able to get my passport for me and help me get out of the country."

"I wouldn't advise that unless you know someone at the Yard you can trust with your life," he said bluntly. "Whoever's after you has a hell of a long reach. If they can hire thugs in England to try to kill you in a car accident, then kidnap you just hours after you return to England, they can hire anyone. Be careful who you trust."

She paled. He was right. Was she willing to take a chance going to the police? What if they refused to let her leave England? And then the press somehow got hold of the story? Her kidnappers would know where she was, and just the thought of that scared the hell out of her.

Suddenly chilled to the bone, she shivered. "No," she said huskily. "You're right. I don't want to take any more chances. Let's go back to the flat."

Finding her passport, however, wasn't as simple as showing up at Priscilla's flat and digging through the Dumpster in the alley. Logic told Donovan that her kidnappers were long gone by now, but if they really did throw her passport in the Dumpster, they knew she'd have to come back for it. And when she did, someone would, in all likelihood, be watching.

They wouldn't, however, see Priscilla Wyatt. "We're changing vehicles," he said abruptly, and headed for one of the numerous car rentals near the airport. "If someone is watching your flat, they'll be looking for the van—and you. We've got to make some changes."

An hour later, after they'd changed to a black Toyota Camry and Donovan made a quick stop at a drugstore that was open all night, he took her to his office on the opposite side of town. When he managed to whisk her inside without a single soul seeing her, she should have been relieved. Instead, she couldn't stop thinking about the "changes" Donovan intended to implement. Just what did he have in mind?

She found out almost immediately when he retrieved a pair of scissors from the bag of mysterious items he'd bought at the drugstore. She took one look at them and dug in her heels. "If you think you're going to cut my hair, you can think again, mister. It's not happening."

He gave her a wounded look. "This isn't my first rodeo, sweetheart. I've cut a woman's hair before."

"And she lived to tell about it?"

"Last I heard, she was still kicking." He chuckled. "And, I might add, she's still wearing her hair the way I cut it."

For a moment, Priscilla *almost* believed him. Then she saw the glint of mischief in his eyes. "You're good," she said with reluctant admiration. "Too good. I'll keep my hair, thank you very much."

"It'll grow back—"

"Easy for you to say," she cut in. "I don't see you letting me cut yours."

Without a word, he held the scissors out to her.

Surprised, she studied him suspiciously. "Are you serious?"

"Like I said, sweet cakes, it grows back. Take your best shot. Do it right, and my own mother won't recognize me."

It would serve him right if she took him at his word, she thought. But then again, he might do the same thing to her. Hesitating, she eyed him warily. "Is that what you're going to do to me?"

He grinned wickedly. "You'll have to wait and find out. But I'll give you this, though—if you don't like it, you can pull out every hair on my body with tweezers and laugh when you do it."

Her lips twitched. "Don't tempt me, Donovan. That just might make up for everything you've put me through."

"I'm at your mercy, Prissy. Just remember, I'm only trying to keep you safe."

She could no longer argue with that. He had saved her twice from her kidnappers and in the process, put his own life at risk. "I know," she said softly, "and I appreciate that. I'm sorry I caused you so much trouble."

"Just remember that the next time you want to kill me," he said with a grin. Pulling out a chair from the small table and chairs in the office kitchen, he sat down with his back to her and stretched out his long legs. "Do your worst, sweetheart. Whatever you do, I'll survive."

She took him at his word—but she didn't use the scissors. Instead, she retrieved an electric men's all-in-one groomer from the bag of supplies from the drugstore and proceeded to give him a military buzz cut. And even though he had to know what she was doing, he didn't issue a single word of complaint.

When she was finished, Priscilla was almost afraid to look at the finished result. Then Donovan rubbed his head and laughed. "All right! Is this cool or what?"

Priscilla considered him with a reluctant grin. "Actually, you look like a marine. And you got what you wanted. I don't think your own mother would recognize you."

"Great! Now it's your turn."

Her stomach in a knot, Priscilla clutched the scissors to her breast. "I don't know. Maybe this isn't such a good idea, after all."

"Oh, no, you don't," he said quickly, and grabbed

the scissors out of her hand before she could guess his intentions. "A deal's a deal."

"But—"

"Don't even try to tell me you're backing out. You're not the kind of woman who gives her word then backs out."

Surprised, she blinked. "How do you know what kind of woman I am? You don't even know me."

"I know you well enough to know that you're a fighter, that you love your family and hate injustice. A woman like that isn't going to go back on her word to a man who is trying to protect her."

He had her, and they both knew it. Caught in the trap of his steady blue gaze, she knew she had to trust him. "All right," she said, and sank down into the chair he'd just vacated. Then, before he could touch a hair on her head, she looked up at him worriedly. "You're not going to shave my head, are you?"

A half smile tilted up one corner of his mouth. "You wouldn't look nearly as cute as I do bald," he teased. "Your hair is safe with me."

She had to believe him—he hadn't lied to her yet. Still, she found it hard to relax as he started to cut her hair. When her pulse tripped, she tried to tell herself she was just nervous—any woman would be. But she knew it was more than that. It was the feel of his hands in her hair, the unconsciously provocative stroke of his fingers on the back of her neck, that was setting her heart pounding.

She should be worried about her hair, she told herself. Instead, all she could think about was Donovan…his nearness, the masculine scent of him, his fingers moving over her—

"All finished," he announced suddenly. "Take a look."

Before she even looked at herself in the bathroom mirror, she lifted a hand to her hair. It was short, barely reaching her collar, and a mass of loose curls. How many years had she been straightening her naturally curly hair? When was the last time she'd had it cut? She couldn't remember.

"You look like Meg Ryan," he told her, grinning. "Only cuter."

She didn't believe that for a second—until she looked in the mirror and saw a woman she barely recognized. The cut could only be called ragged, at best, but it wasn't much different from some of the expensive salon cuts that some of her friends wore. And she was surprised to discover that she actually liked the curls. They were bouncy, touchable, feminine.

Standing behind her, his gaze meeting hers in the mirror, Donovan grinned. "We make quite a pair, Ms. Prissy. But we're not done yet."

Surprised, she frowned. "What do you mean? You said yourself your own mother wouldn't recognize you. And I know I could walk right by the jackasses who kidnapped me and they wouldn't look twice at me like this."

"We're going to take it one step further and make sure," he said, and pulled out two boxes of hair dye from the bag of supplies from the drugstore. "One for each of us," he said with a grin. "Take your pick, sweetheart. Do you want to be a redhead or a brunette?"

Ideally, Donovan would have liked nothing more than to head back to her apartment and search the

Dumpster in the dark. But they'd need a flashlight to find her passport, and anyone watching for them would spot them in a heartbeat. So they rested for what was left of the night, and even though Priscilla eventually fell asleep on the couch in the waiting area, Donovan didn't. He was too busy making plans.

Four hours later, when Donovan drove across town to Priscilla's flat, he had to admit he was pleased. They looked nothing like the couple who'd checked into the motel hours before. Dressed in torn jeans and a faded, ragged shirt, army boots and a skullcap that was pulled down low over his short red hair, he looked like a homeless man without a penny to his name. And Priscilla looked just as bad.

When he'd first told her he wanted her to dress like a bag lady, he'd expected her to balk at the idea, but she'd thrown herself into the role, starting with the clothes she bought at a thrift store down the block from his office. Three sizes too big, she put at least three different mismatched outfits on at one time, then topped it all with an overcoat that had to be thirty years old and would have swallowed a woman twice her size. Then she'd surprised him by rubbing dirt on her face.

Her kidnappers would never recognize her, Donovan decided, grinning. She could search every Dumpster in the neighborhood and no one would give her a second glance. Still, he wasn't taking any chances.

"I want you to stay in the car," he said gruffly as he parked around the corner from her flat. Pulling a business card from his wallet, he handed it to her. "If I'm not back in ten minutes, I want you to drive to

Scotland Yard and ask for George Hudson. Tell him I sent you and what's happened."

"*Stay in the car?!*" she repeated, stunned. "Are you serious?"

"You're damn straight," he growled.

"Why? What was the point of cutting my hair and having me dress like a street woman if I have to hide out in the car?"

"So one of your neighbors won't recognize you if they happen to see you."

"That doesn't explain why I have to stay in the car. If no one's going to recognize me, I might as well go with you."

"They'll be looking for a woman," he reminded her. "If you're in the car and they happen to spot you, at least you can drive away. You can't do that if you're on foot."

"But—"

"This isn't open for discussion," he said firmly. "You're staying in the car."

Her chin came up at his tone—she didn't need his permission to search for her own passport. But even as she gave serious consideration to doing what she damn well pleased, she knew he was right. Her kidnappers were clever and fast. If their path crossed hers, they'd catch her before she could even think about making a break for it.

"I'm staying because it's the smart thing to do," she told him, irritated. "That's the only reason."

He didn't care what reasoning she used as long as she did as she was told. "Remember…ten minutes, then you head for Scotland Yard. I'll find you."

She wanted to argue—he could see it in her eyes—

but she only nodded. Fighting the sudden crazy urge to kiss her, he reached for her hand and squeezed it. A split second later, he was gone.

Almost immediately, time seemed to slow to a crawl. Worried sick, she checked her watch. How long had he been gone? A couple of minutes? Had he found the Dumpster behind her apartment? Surely he had, but then again, he couldn't hurry. He was a homeless man who had nothing but time on his hands. If he hurried, someone would surely ask why.

How did he do this for a living? she wondered wildly. It was too nerve-racking, too stressful. Wasn't he afraid her kidnappers would see through his disguise and come after him? If they were watching, they were bound to see him. And they were watching. She could feel them.

Sick to her stomach with fear, she tried to convince herself that her imagination was just playing tricks on her. She was well hidden behind the Camry's dark windows—no one could possibly see her. And even if they could, they wouldn't recognize her. So why was she suddenly so scared?

Unable to sit still a second longer, she checked her watch and felt her heart stop cold. Where was Donovan? He'd been gone fifteen minutes!

If I'm not back in ten minutes, I want you to drive to Scotland Yard...

Even as his words replayed in her head, she knew she couldn't do it. She couldn't drive off and leave him in the hands of whoever had stopped him from keeping his word. Was he hurt? Maybe she should go looking for him—

Caught up in her worried thoughts, she never saw Donovan slip up on the rental car from the rear. When he opened the door with the second set of keys the rental company had given him, she nearly jumped out of her skin.

"Get down in the floorboard," Donovan commanded as he slipped into the seat beside her. With a quick flick of his wrist, he started the car. "Now!" he barked when she just sat there. "We may have company."

He didn't have to tell her twice. Lightning quick, she dropped into the floorboard as he pulled away from the curb. "What do you mean...*we may have company? Who*—"

His gaze bouncing between the road in front of them and the rearview mirror, he said, "There was a bloke near the entrance to the alley acting like he was waiting for a bus. But he never got on any of the buses that came by."

"He didn't see you go into the alley, did he?"

"No, but only because he was distracted by the jackass who broke into your flat just as I walked into the alley."

"What?!"

"You heard me," he said grimly. "Somebody broke into your apartment."

"Did you see him? What'd he look like?"

His eyes on the road, he nodded. "It was one of your friends."

Surprised, she frowned. "A friend? What friend? You don't know any of my friends."

"I know this one. It was one of your kidnappers."

Chapter 5

They drove all day and into the night. Horrified that her kidnappers were still looking for her, Priscilla didn't even bother to ask where Donovan was taking her. It wasn't until they crossed into Scotland that she realized they were going to Edinburgh. They didn't, however, head for the airport, as she'd expected. Instead, Donovan drove deeper and deeper into the city, making sudden turns, then backtracking, down a maze of ancient streets that were progressively narrower, darker, scarier.

When he pulled up before a small inn that looked like it had to be home to nothing but drug dealers and cockroaches, she looked at him like he'd lost his mind. "Tell me you're not expecting to spend what's left of the night here."

Amused, he lifted a masculine brow at her in the

darkness. "That was my intention. Why? You want to stay longer than one night?"

"That's not funny," she snapped, giving him a withering look. "Decent people don't stay in a place like this."

"They do when they have kidnappers chasing them," he retorted. "Trust me, no one's going to look for a woman like you here with the hookers. C'mon."

Not giving her a chance to argue further, he stepped from the car and waited for her to join him. The second she did, he took her hand. Confused, she frowned. "What are you doing?"

"Just keeping you safe," he said with a grin and pulled her into the inn after him.

The desk clerk was half asleep and staring at the television, where an erotic video played for anyone who walked in the door to see. Repulsed, Priscilla wanted to turn around and walk out, but Donovan stopped her in her tracks with his first words. "We need a room."

Caught off guard, she looked at him sharply. "Excuse me? *A* room? As in *one*? You can't be serious—"

Donovan had to shut her up and he had to do it fast. There was no time to think, no time to do anything but act. Pasting a teasing grin on, he reached for her. "Don't be that way, sweetheart. You know you love me." And before she could do anything but gasp, he covered her mouth with his.

She wanted to kill him—he could almost hear her cursing him as she stiffened and brought up her hands to push him away. Then, just as quickly, she hesitated. Thank God, she'd finally remembered she was supposed to follow his lead, he thought. Then she kissed him back.

Lightning came out of nowhere to knock him out of his shoes.

Caught off guard, he felt the punch of desire in his gut and just barely swallowed a groan. They were playing a part, he reminded himself. Pretending. The last thing he wanted was the desk clerk wondering why Priscilla would object to sharing a room with him when they came in together, so he'd kissed her in the hope that the man would think they were just two lovers who'd had a spat. The last thing he'd expected was that she would kiss him back...or that she would turn him inside out when she did.

"All right, all right." The desk clerk smirked. "I guess it's one room, after all."

"You're damn straight," Donovan muttered, releasing Priscilla with a reluctance that stunned him. "And be quick about it."

Pulling out his wallet, he slid a credit card across the desk to the other man and registered the room in the name of one of his favorite aliases. Seconds later, he and Priscilla headed for their room.

She was just itching to say something—he could feel her impatience as he unlocked the door and she preceded him inside. The second the door closed, she blasted him. "How dare you! You had no right!"

"The hell I didn't! It's my job to protect you, even from yourself, and there was no other way to shut you up when the desk clerk was listening to every word we said."

"You should have warned me ahead of time."

"I agree," he said. "That was my mistake. I should

have told you this isn't the kind of place where you want to stay alone. I can't protect you if I'm not with you."

Far from appeased, she gave him a narrow-eyed look that would have had another man shaking in his shoes. "I'm not sharing a bed with you."

"Have it your way," he said with a shrug. "But you don't know what you're missing."

"I'm sure I'll survive the disappointment," she said dryly. "Now if you'll excuse me, I'm going to take a shower and go to bed. You can sleep on the floor."

Sailing into the bathroom with her chin in the air, she shut the door behind her, but her feelings of victory were short-lived. She took one look at the small bathroom and cringed. The shower stall was rough with lime buildup, and the rough towels folded on the towel rack were dingy and thin with age. Priscilla didn't even want to think about how many times they'd been used and by whom.

Revolted at the thought, she almost turned and walked out, but she was tired and dirty and could still smell the scent of her kidnappers on her skin. She was, by God, going to have a shower, but there was no way she was letting one of those nasty towels touch her skin. She'd air dry.

When she stepped out of the bathroom fifteen minutes later dressed in some of her bag lady clothes, Donovan was in the process of stripping the sheets from the bed and turning the mattress over. When she stopped in surprise, she would have sworn he blushed. "Okay, so it's not the Ritz," he said with a grimace. "I'm sorry I had to bring you here—it's no place for a lady. But it's the best I can do for now and still keep you safe."

Touched, Priscilla didn't know if she wanted to laugh or cry. She hadn't expected him to be so thoughtful. "It'll be fine," she said huskily. "Thank you."

"No problem," he said with a shrug. Removing his pistol from his overnight bag, he laid it on the nightstand. "It's loaded," he told her. "While I'm in the shower, don't be afraid to use it if there's a problem."

She couldn't—just the thought of picking it up turned her blood cold—but all she said was, "I'm sure I'll be fine."

She didn't fool him for a second. "You're so full of—"

"Donovan!"

"You are," he repeated, grinning. "Just promise me you'll come and get me if someone's at the door, okay?"

Eyeing him suspiciously, she said, "Are you trying to scare me? Because if you are, you're doing a good job of it."

"Good. You need to be scared. You've got some bad dudes chasing you. You can't afford to forget it."

She wasn't likely to forget it, she thought as he disappeared into the bathroom to take a shower. She was in an inn she normally wouldn't be caught dead in, with a man she hardly knew. And there was a loaded gun on the nightstand. No, she hadn't forgotten anything, least of all that there were strangers trying to find her who wouldn't blink twice if they were given the order to kill her.

Suddenly cold all the way to her soul, she crawled into bed, clothes and all. She was so tired, she felt like the walking dead, but she wasn't surprised when she found herself wide awake. Was that a step she heard outside in the hallway? Her heart suddenly in her throat, she reminded herself that the building was ancient and probably creaked every time the wind blew…or a mouse peaked out of its hole.

Paling at the thought, she sat up, her eyes searching the dark corners of the room. What if it wasn't a mouse at all, but a rat? "Oh, God."

The bathroom door opened then, and Donovan stepped out dressed in nothing but his jeans. Rubbing his wet hair with one of the dingy towels she hadn't been able to bring herself to use, he looked like he'd just walked out of one of her fantasies…and all she could think of was rats.

"What's wrong?" he demanded, seeing her face.

"I heard a noise in the hallway," she said, trembling.

"What kind of noise?"

She shrugged. "I don't know. It wasn't very loud. It could have been a mouse—"

"Or a rat," he said casually, then crossed to the nightstand to grab his gun. "I'll check it out."

He stepped out into the hallway before she could stop him, alarming her. He didn't even look out the peephole. What if her kidnappers were out there, waiting for him? He could be dead before he could blink.

"Wait!" she cried. "Someone could be out there—"

Scrambling after him, she only just missed plowing into him as he stepped back into their room. Grinning, he pressed a hand to his heart. "Why, Prissy, I didn't know you cared."

"Don't flatter yourself," she sniffed. Turning her back on him, she said, "I'm going to bed."

"Good idea," he said, and strode past her to the bed.

Stunned, Priscilla couldn't believe it when he sank down onto the far side of the bed. "What are you doing? I'm sleeping there!"

"Fine," he retorted with a grin, and scooted over. "I'll take the other side."

"No! Damn it, Donovan, I told you—" she began indignantly, only to forget what she was going to say next when she felt something on her bare foot. Surprised, she glanced down…and screamed at the sight of the roach crawling across her foot. "Aaagh!"

"What the hell?!" Lightning quick, Donovan jumped off the bed just as she threw herself at him. "What is it?" he demanded, snatching her close. "What's wrong?"

"A roach!" she gasped. "There was a roach on my foot!"

If she hadn't been so obviously upset, Donovan would have laughed. *A roach?* She was terrified of a roach? "It's not going to hurt you," he assured her. "Sit still and I'll kill it."

Switching on every light in the room, he saw the roach almost immediately and stepped on it as it headed for the door. Seconds later, he disposed of it in the bathroom, then returned to the bedroom to find Priscilla sitting in the middle of the bed and nervously searching the room for more roaches.

Suppressing a smile, he said, "It's okay—you can relax. The big, bad roach is dead. Now can we go to sleep?"

She stiffened. "What do you mean…*we?*"

"I'm going to bed," he said simply, and slipped into bed beside her. And before she could do anything but gasp, he stretched out on his stomach, punched the pillow under his head and sighed in contentment.

Beside him, he could almost feel Priscilla's irritation. She didn't, however, find somewhere else to sleep. Instead, she used the headboard as a backrest and stretched her legs out in front of her. Apparently, she intended to sit up the rest of the night rather than lie down next to him.

Her choice, he told himself. He wasn't going to lose any sleep over it.

But sleeping while she sat next to him in bed wasn't nearly as easy as he'd anticipated. Aware of every breath she took, every sigh, every shift of her body as she tried to get comfortable, he couldn't seem to think of anything but her as he lay there. Seconds passed, minutes, a half hour. And somehow, even with his eyes closed and his head turned away from her, he knew the exact moment she fell asleep.

A selfish man would have left her as she was and caught some shut-eye himself. But his mother had raised him better than that, and when he turned toward her, he wasn't surprised to find her slumped to the side, her head at an awkward angle. Telling himself she was going to owe him for this, he gently eased her down on the bed.

The second he touched her, he knew he'd made a mistake. She was too soft, too vulnerable, and when she sighed in her sleep and curled toward him, all he could think about was reaching for her, pulling her toward him, kissing her awake.

Silently swearing, he forced himself to turn away from her, but for what seemed like hours, he lay there, listening to her breathe, wanting her, imagining too damn much. Irritated, he told himself he must be getting soft. He didn't want anything to do with a woman, and he had Jennifer to thank for that.

Images stirred, images he'd locked away a long time ago. Silently swallowing a curse, he slammed the door shut on the memories of the only woman he'd ever loved and focused instead on the lesson she'd taught him. Don't trust a woman...ever. Because when push came to shove, she wouldn't stand by you when you needed her the most.

Not all women are alike.

Grimacing at the too-wise voice that whispered in his head, he had to admit that might be a possibility, but that was beside the point. He knew better than to get involved with his customers, especially one like Priscilla Wyatt. She was too prissy, too snooty, too delicate...and he could still taste her on his tongue.

He never should have kissed her, he decided. It had been a dumb thing to do. He could have come up with a quick lie about them having a lovers' spat, and the desk clerk wouldn't have thought twice about the two of them getting separate rooms. Instead, he'd reached for her to shut her up, and now all he could think about was kissing her again.

He was losing his mind, he decided glumly. There was no other explanation. Buck had hired him to kidnap his sister and keep her safe. That was it. There'd been no mention of kissing her, seducing her, sleeping with her. If he had a brain in his head, he'd give her the bed and sleep on the floor.

He considered the idea for all of five seconds, but

the carpet was filthier than the bed. He was being ridiculous, he decided. He was so tired, Priscilla could have been snuggled flush against his back and it wouldn't have mattered. He couldn't keep his eyes open any longer. He settled into a more comfortable position, and seconds later, he was asleep.

Priscilla slipped into his dreams uninvited, and not surprisingly, the stubborn woman refused to leave him alone. She teased him with her smile, with a touch that no man with any blood in his veins could possibly resist, then danced away with a laugh when he reached for her. Hot, aching for her, he promised himself when he got his hands on her that he wouldn't let her go until she begged him for release.

Caught deep in the depths of his tantalizing dream, Donovan couldn't have said what planet he was on, let alone what city he slept in. It didn't matter. Nothing mattered but the woman in his dreams who was doing her best to drive him out of his mind.

Then a gun exploded right outside their room.

Instantly awake, Donovan never remembered moving. One second, he was sound asleep, the next, his pistol was in his hand and he was on his feet, braced for whatever was outside the door to their room.

"Priscilla? Get up!"

Buried under the bedspread, she didn't move. "Hmm?"

"Get up," he commanded again. "I just heard a gunshot outside."

That got her attention. *What?!*" Struggling out from under the covers, her hair a mass of short wild curls and her eyes dark with confusion, she pushed herself into a sitting position and frowned up at him. "Are you serious?"

He nodded urgently. "C'mon—move. I want you to go into the bathroom and lock the door. Regardless of what you hear, don't come out until I tell you it's safe. Understood?"

"Of course." Pale and shaken, she scrambled off the bed and hurried into the bathroom.

In the tense silence, the click of the door being locked was as loud as a scream. His lean, rugged face set in grim lines, Donovan hurriedly slipped on his boots and, as silently as possible, unlocked the dead bolt on the door to their room. Seconds later, with his gun drawn and his senses on high alert, he stepped soundlessly into the hallway.

Fear gripping her by the throat, Priscilla pressed an ear to the bathroom door, but she couldn't hear anything but the furious pounding of her heart. Was Donovan still in their room or had he already left? Maybe he should have called the police, she thought. At least then he'd have some kind of backup. As it was, he was fighting the bad guys all by himself.

She tried to tell herself that he was clever. This wasn't his first rodeo, as he'd reminded her, and he had plenty of experience. Chasing the scum of the earth was what he did for a living. She couldn't imagine anyone catching him off guard.

So why was she worried about a man who could obviously take care of himself?

Because anyone could make a mistake, she thought,

fear twisting in her gut. And while he was out there in the hall, putting his life on the line for her, she was cowering in the bathroom.

Cringing at the thought, she knew she had to do something, but she didn't have a clue what when she unlocked the bathroom door. She just knew she couldn't let Donovan face her demons alone.

She hurried to the door, but before she could even reach for it, it swung open sharply. Startled, she gasped, a scream already building inside her, only to find herself face-to-face with Donovan.

"Thank God!" she said. "I've been so worried!"

"You're supposed to be locked in the bathroom," he growled, scowling as he shot the dead bolt home.

"I was, but—"

"But what? Dammit, Prissy, are you trying to get yourself killed? I specifically told you to stay in the bathroom!"

"I was worried about you," she exclaimed, heat climbing in her cheeks. "I was afraid you were hurt."

"So you're going to ignore orders and put yourself in danger, too?" he demanded. "Is that what you're saying?"

Her green eyes snapped fire at his assumption that she was supposed to follow orders. "No, of course not," she said stiffly. "But what was I supposed to do? Stay in the bathroom, where I was nice and safe, while you were possibly being attacked? Do you really think I'm the kind of person who would do that?

"Don't answer that," she said quickly before he could say a word. "It doesn't matter what you think. I did what I had to do. If my actions don't meet with your approval, then I guess that's too damn bad."

"Now don't get all huffy on me—"

"Huffy?" She sniffed. "Of course I'm huffy! Excuse me for breathing…or thinking of someone besides myself while you stick your neck out for me. Maybe you should have kidnapped someone else, some self-centered princess who wouldn't have cared less what happened to you as long as she was safe."

For a moment, she thought she saw his lips twitch, but one glare from her and he immediately sobered. "Look," he said, sighing, "I didn't mean to hurt your feelings—"

"Well, you did!"

"I know you were only trying to help me, and I appreciate that. But you're the one the bad guys are after, sweetheart, not me. I can't keep either one of us safe if you're not where you're supposed to be."

"I was *trying* to help."

"Next time, do as you're told, and we'll get along fine."

Her eyes narrowed dangerously. "Excuse me? Did you say *do as I'm told?*"

"You're damn straight I did," he said flatly. "If that's a problem, then tell me now. I'll call Buck and tell him this isn't going to work and he might as well turn the family ranch over to whoever's orchestrating all this, because you're going to lose it anyway."

Shocked, she gasped. "What? You can't be serious!"

"Every time you work against me instead of with me, you're putting yourself and the ranch in jeopardy. And one of these times, someone is going to grab you. I'll find you," he promised grimly, "but I don't know that I'll find you in time."

He didn't have to explain what he meant by that—she understood him perfectly. Next time she might be dead. Guilt tugging at her for causing him so much trouble, she said, "I'm sorry. I wasn't thinking. It won't happen again. From now on, I'll do what you say."

He lifted a brow at her. "Even when you want to kill me?"

"I never—" she began, only to see the twinkle in his eyes. "That could change," she warned, trying and failing to bite back a smile. "If you keep pushing me…"

"Oh, c'mon," he teased. "You love it and you know it. It keeps your mind off what's going on at the ranch."

Sobering, she couldn't deny it. "These last few months have been horrible," she said quietly. "The family's kept me posted on what's been going on in Colorado, but that's not the same thing as being there. Up until now, I've only been able to imagine how frightening it's been for them, being under constant attack. Now that I know what it's like, I understand why they're so worried about me. And there's nothing I can do about it. I can't even manage to get to the States."

"Don't give up yet," he told her. "I've got a plan."

She'd heard that before. Eyeing him warily, she said, "Why don't I like the sound of that?"

"You'll love it," he said, chuckling. "I promise."

Six hours later, when Priscilla walked into the Edinburgh airport, her legs were anything but steady and her heart was threatening to beat out of her chest. Donovan had assured her that he would be within sight at all times, but she didn't see him anywhere, and she'd never been more scared in her life. Were her kidnappers there somewhere, waiting for her? Would they recognize her?

Sick to her stomach, she almost lifted a hand to her short curly hair. She'd been afraid that the new haircut and dye job wouldn't be enough to disguise her looks, so Donovan had bought her a striped hoodie and pencil thin black pants and ballerina slippers. With oversized sunglasses, she looked like a young Audrey Hepburn. Her stride graceful and easy, she reminded herself that she was supposed to be acting like a jet-setter who knew exactly where she was going. She couldn't let anyone who was watching suspect that she was scared out of her mind and wanted to run to the nearest policeman.

Donovan wouldn't let anything happen to her, she assured herself as she headed for the ticket counter. The plan he'd concocted was for each of them to buy their ticket separately, then end up at the same gate like they were perfect strangers. And since they were both using aliases and passports that he had doctored, no one would, hopefully, realize they were traveling together.

In theory, it sounded good. But her knees knocked at the idea of using her doctored passport. And before she could join the line at the ticket counter, someone suddenly bumped into her from the right. Her passport went flying, as did his. "Oh! I'm sorry—"

Instinctively, she kneeled down to pick up her passport and just that quickly, found herself down on her knees with the man who had bumped into her. "Are you all right?" he asked and it was only then that she realized that man was Donovan.

Startled, she glanced up. They weren't supposed to

have any contact until they landed in Monaco, which was the first flight out that morning. "What—"

"Keep picking up your things," he said quietly, not looking at her. "There's been a change of plans. Monaco's out."

With trembling fingers, she reached for her passport. "Why?"

"There are two thugs watching everyone who goes through security," he said in a whisper that didn't carry beyond her ears. "One's by the big plant at eleven o'clock, and the other one is pretending to read a newspaper near the newsstand, which is across the concourse over my right shoulder. Easy!" he said quickly when she started to check out the two men. "Look at me. Then check them out without moving your head. They won't be able to tell you're looking at them because of your sunglasses."

Her heart threatening to beat out of her chest, she did as he said and spotted the two men almost immediately. Surprised, she almost dropped her things again. "They're not my kidnappers."

"Are you sure?"

"Absolutely. I've never seen either one of them before."

Donovan swore softly as he rose to his feet and helped her up. "We still can't chance that they're not looking for you. Go to the restroom, wait a few minutes, then go back to the front entrance and wait for me at the curb. I'll be there in five minutes."

He didn't give her a chance to say anything else and simply walked away. Their chance encounter over, she headed for the restroom without sparing a glance for the two men who were obviously watching for someone. Had they been sent by her kidnappers to watch for her? she wondered, shaken. How many others were out there, watching? Waiting for a chance to grab her when she least expected it? How could she protect herself when she didn't even know who to protect herself from?

She finally reached the restroom, but she found little comfort there. There was no guarantee that her kidnappers had just sent men after her. What if one of the women who strolled in after her had been sent to kill her? Was the blonde looking at her as she washed her hands capable of murder? What about the tall brunette? Could she be a man in drag?

Paranoid from the suspicious thoughts racing through her mind, she didn't glance at her watch to see if five minutes had passed. She didn't care—she had to get out of there. Struggling not to hurry, she headed for the front entrance, half expecting someone to stop her any second, but no one did. And just as she reached the curb, Donovan pulled up in the rental car. Relieved, she reached for the door handle before he'd even braked to a complete stop.

"Thank God!" Slipping into the car beside him, she slammed her door and locked it as he pulled away from the curb. "Now what do we do?"

His eyes trained on the rearview mirror, he said, "Try another airport."

"Where?"

"Manchester."

Chapter 6

By the time they turned south and reached Manchester, England, Priscilla was so exhausted that she couldn't see straight. All she wanted to do was get a room and go to bed. Donovan, however, wouldn't even consider it.

"We're taking the first flight out," he told her, pulling into the long-term parking lot. "I'll go in first. Then you follow five minutes later. Go to the restroom while I check outgoing flights and find out what the next flight out is. Watch for me when you come out of the restroom, and try to make sure you're not right behind me at the ticket counter. Then we're on our way."

He made it sound so simple. Her heart rattling in her chest, she eyed the entrance warily. The place looked deserted. "Maybe we should wait until a little later in the morning, when there are more people around," she said. "If someone's here, watching for us, they're going to sit up and take notice the second we both walk in within five minutes of each other."

"First of all, I'm not walking in by myself. It's still really early. Give it another fifteen minutes, and this place is going to get pretty frantic. When the parking garage starts filling up, I'll walk in with some other passengers and no one will look twice at me." He gave her a pointed look. "If you do the same thing, this should be a cakewalk. And remember, you don't look anything like you did, and you're using an alias. You're going to be fine."

Far from convinced, she stared at him doubtfully. "And what if someone grabs you the minute you walk into the terminal?"

"Then I have a problem," he retorted. "You don't because you're not coming in until I call you."

When he handed her his phone, she asked nervously, "And if you don't call?"

"Then you get the hell out of here and head for the local office of Scotland Yard or the U.S. Embassy, whichever one you can find first," he responded. "And call Buck the first chance you get."

"And just leave you? You can't be serious."

"You have to," he said firmly. "Your life is at stake. Remember? And I can take care of myself."

Not giving her a chance to argue further, he looked in the rearview mirror and said, "Things are starting to pick up. That's my cue. Just follow the plan, and I'll see you inside." And before she could guess his intentions, he leaned across the console and kissed her.

It wasn't like the kiss he'd given her for the hotel

clerk's benefit—hot and passionate and overwhelming. Instead, he kissed her slowly, sweetly, so softly that she felt like she was floating. If she hadn't known better, she would have sworn she imagined the whole thing. But her heart rolled over in her breast, her pulse was throbbing and she was totally entranced.

Mindless, boneless, she leaned toward him, aching for another kiss, but he was gone almost immediately, leaving her alone and longing for something she'd only dreamed of finding in this lifetime.

Later, she couldn't say how long she sat there, unable to think of anything but the pounding of her heart and the man who was responsible for it. Did he know how easily he stole the breath right out of her lungs? Did she do the same to him?

The phone rang then, startling her out of her musings. Sending up a silent prayer of thanks that he wasn't there to see the heat coloring her cheeks, she snatched it up. "H-hello?"

If he noticed her voice was husky and more than a little unsteady, he made no comment. Instead, he said, "It's all clear, Pris. It's safe to come in."

"Are you sure?"

"Absolutely. There's no one in here but a couple of families. You're safe."

If circumstances had been different, she might have laughed. *Safe?* How could she be safe when he threatened her peace of mind, not to mention her heart? She wanted to run halfway across the world, but she knew it wouldn't be far enough. What was he doing to her?

Refusing to let her mind go there, she locked the car and forced herself to walk into the airport with a confidence she was far from feeling. The second she stepped inside, she saw Donovan from the corner of her eye. He was standing in the short line in front of the British Airways ticket counter. As she headed for it, a woman with a toddler stepped into line behind him. Relieved, Priscilla crossed the terminal and got in line behind the mother and toddler.

Donovan didn't spare her a glance, but Priscilla wasn't fooled. Anyone as sharp as he was had to have eyes in the back of his head. He knew exactly what was going on all around him.

Ten minutes later, she'd cleared the first hurdle. The ticket agent had checked her passport and hadn't so much as blinked at the sight of her doctored passport. She wasn't, however, in the clear yet. She still had to make it through security.

Nearly paralyzed with fear, she headed for the security checkpoint and never saw Donovan heading in the same direction until his path intersected hers. His gaze focused on his ticket, he plowed into her, knocking her purse off her shoulder and her ticket and passport out of her hand.

"Oh!"

"Oh, geez, I'm sorry! Are you hurt?"

"N-no," she stuttered. "I'm fine. Really."

"Thank God! I was so stupid—I wasn't looking where I was going. Here…let me help you pick up your things."

He dropped down to one knee as she squatted to pick up her things. Her heart lurched at the sight of his smile and the wicked twinkle in his eyes. Oh, he was enjoying himself! "What are you doing?" she hissed. "You're not supposed to talk to me until we're on the plane."

"Can't a man flirt with a pretty lady?" he teased.

"Someone will see," she said under her breath, "and think we're together."

"Not when we didn't come in together," he said. "Now I can ask whoever's sitting next to you to change places with me and they'll just think I'm hitting on you."

Rolling her eyes, she tried not to smile. "You're incorrigible."

"Guilty as charged," he said, and helped her to her feet. Then, in a slightly louder voice, he said in a thick Texas accent, "Can I buy you breakfast, miss, while you wait for your plane? A pretty little lady like you shouldn't have to eat breakfast alone."

Reminding herself she was playing a role, she exclaimed, "Oh, I can't! My husband wouldn't like it. He's very possessive. He wouldn't even want me talking to you. Excuse me. I have to go."

"Well, damn, honey, you need to leave his ass and get yourself an easygoing fella like me."

Her eyes lowered to hide the laughter she knew was reflected there. She turned and hurried to the security check.

She knew without looking that Donovan followed at a more leisurely pace, and she was thankful for his nearness as she stepped out of her shoes and set her purse on the conveyor belt to be x-rayed. Although she half expected security to give her passport a second look, the guard only waved her through, then Donovan as he got behind her in line.

Not sure if she wanted to laugh or cry, Priscilla didn't dare look back at Donovan as he followed her down the concourse to their gate. With a sigh of relief, she saw that the rest of the passengers were already boarding the plane. Presenting her ticket to the flight attendant, she walked right onto the plane with Donovan two steps behind her.

Not surprisingly, their seats weren't together, but Donovan didn't let that present a problem. When he saw that Priscilla's seat was toward the rear of the plane, he approached her seat companion, an elderly woman who was old enough to be her grandmother, and grinned. "Excuse me, ma'am, but could I convince you to change seats with me? I'd really like to get to know this little lady a whole lot better, if you don't mind."

Far from impressed with him, she only said tartly, "It isn't a question of whether I mind, young man, but whether *she* does." Glancing at Priscilla, she lifted a gray brow over faded blue eyes sharp with amusement. "Do you want to talk to this scamp, young lady? He seems awfully sure of himself."

Heat climbing in her cheeks, Priscilla smiled. "He is outrageous, isn't he? But I really would like to talk to him."

"Somehow I knew you would say that," she replied, chuckling as she gathered her things and rose to her feet. "I remember what it was like to flirt with a scamp. Have fun."

Grinning, Donovan slipped into the seat she'd just vacated and reached for Priscilla's hand. "Nice work, Pris. Talk about a cool customer! If I didn't know better, I'd have sworn you've been doing this for years."

With a will of their own, her fingers curled around his, and she was too elated to care. For the first time since she'd been kidnapped, she felt safe. "I did do pretty good," she said, more than a little pleased with herself. "So where are we going?"

Grinning, he leaned back and closed his eyes. "Budapest. Wake me when we get there."

If circumstances had been different, Donovan would have liked nothing more than to explore Budapest and its centuries-old streets with Priscilla, but there was no time. They may have managed to escape from England and her kidnappers, but he knew better than to drop his guard. So the second they landed and walked off the plane, he guided Priscilla to the ticket counter and purchased tickets for the next flight out. Forty minutes later, they were on their way to Los Angeles.

It was a long trip. When they landed on US soil more than twenty hours after they'd left Scotland, Priscilla was pale as a ghost and obviously exhausted. She was, though, a hell of a good sport, Donovan acknowledged. She didn't utter a word of complaint when he told her he was renting a car because they weren't staying in Los Angeles. Instead, she joined him in the rental car and kept a sharp lookout to make sure they weren't followed as they left LAX behind and headed for the Pacific Coast Highway.

The traffic moved like lightning down the coast toward San Diego, and Donovan jumped right into the thick of things. He, like Priscilla, was exhausted, but he could find his way home with his eyes closed. And there was nothing he enjoyed more than driving the madness of California freeways. Exhilarated, he wove in and out of the other maniacs on the road and made it to San Diego in record time.

Beside him, Priscilla frowned when he pulled up before his condominium and parked. "What are we doing here?"

"This is where I live," he said simply.

Surprised, she blinked. "I thought you lived in London."

"I have a flat there...and a small place in Brazil. My work takes me all over the world."

"But this is your home base?"

"Most of the time," he agreed, and pushed open the driver's door. "C'mon. I need to get some clothes and some fake IDs with U.S. addresses. How good are you with American accents?"

"Pretty darn good," she said in a perfect Southern drawl as she stepped from the car and joined him on the sidewalk. "Of course, I've always loved New York," she added in a Brooklyn accent that could have fooled a native. "Take your pick."

"I knew there was a reason why I liked you," he said, and unlocked his front door with a flourish. "C'mon in, said the spider to the fly. Make yourself at home. If you're hungry, the kitchen is straight ahead. You might find frozen chicken nuggets in the freezer or some peanut butter in the cabinet—that's about it. Sorry about that."

"That's okay. I'm not really hungry, anyway. I'm too tired."

"I've got to work on the IDs," he told her, "and it could take a while. Why don't you lie down while you're waiting? The bedroom's right past the bathroom. I'll wake you when I'm done."

Normally, she wouldn't have gone anywhere near

his bed, but she was so exhausted, she couldn't resist. Without another word, she headed down the hall and found his bedroom. The second her head hit the pillow, she was dreaming.

Creating fake driver's licenses was something Donovan was particularly good at, and he was quite proud of the aliases he came up with for Priscilla. Mary Jo Culpepper of Savannah, Georgia; Jane Simon of New York City; and Lilly Maverick of Austin, Texas. He hadn't heard her Texas accent, but she was a natural mimic. For her own safety, the quicker she lost her British accent, the better.

Staring at her picture, which he'd copied from her fake passport, he found his thoughts drifting down the hall to his bedroom. He hadn't heard a sound from her in the last hour. Obviously, she liked sleeping in his bed.

The thought teased his senses, making it impossible for him to concentrate. He could see her sprawled across his bed, her dark lashes fanned across her ivory cheeks, her lips softly parted in sleep as she nestled against his pillow. What did she normally wear to bed? he wondered, transfixed. Pajamas? A nightgown? Nothing?

A groan ripped through him at the images that conjured up. He had to stop this! They weren't playing house. This wasn't forever. Once it was safe for her to go home, she would, and he'd once again be alone. And that was just the way he wanted it. He didn't want to have feelings for her, didn't want to make the mistakes with her that he'd made with Jennifer. He didn't want to trust her.

And what difference did it make what she normally

wore to bed? From what he'd seen, it was jeans and T-shirt and, sometimes, even tennis shoes!

And he thanked God for that as he headed down the hall toward his bedroom. Because, right or wrong, he knew that if she'd taken a single thing off, even her shoes, he would have been in trouble.

Stopping in the doorway of his bedroom, he groaned at the sight of Priscilla lying on top of the covers of his bed. She'd taken her shoes off.

He was, he told himself, going to have a talk with her…just as soon as she was out of his bed. But when he stepped over to the bed and shook her by the shoulder, she only moaned and buried her head under *his* pillow. "C'mon, Priscilla, wake up. It's time to leave."

Her only answer was silence.

"Don't do this," he growled. "We need to get out of here."

"No."

Surprised, he frowned. "What?"

"I'm not going anywhere," she said into his mattress. "I have to sleep."

"You can sleep in the car."

Her response was, once again, silence.

"Dammit, Prissy! You can't do this."

She not only could; she did. Even as he watched, she seemed to go boneless right before his eyes, and he realized she'd fallen asleep again.

No! he muttered. He hadn't intended to stay. He certainly hadn't intended to sleep with her. There was always the couch, but dammit, he wasn't going to sleep on the couch in his own home. If Priscilla didn't like it, *she* could sleep on the couch!

Crawling into bed beside her, he had little hope of sleeping. Not with Prissy right beside him and tempting him with every breath she took. He'd just have to suffer through it, he told himself sternly, and hope she woke up before he did something stupid…like reach for her. Why did she have to look so soft and touchable when she was sleeping? he wondered, unable to take his eyes off her. She was making this impossible, and she didn't even know it!

Frustrated, he turned his back on her, but it didn't help. He heard her sigh in her sleep and felt her move into a more comfortable position. Then her bare foot innocently brushed his. There was nothing innocent about his response.

He counted sheep, mentally checked the files of every arrest he'd ever made and went over the birthdays of every member of his family. It didn't help. Then, without even knowing when it happened, he fell asleep.

Three hours later, he woke to find Priscilla still sound asleep…and in his arms. Groggy from sleep, his defenses nonexistent, he groaned. This was not a good idea, he told himself. He needed to put her from him and get the hell out of bed. Now! But how the devil was he supposed to do that when she was pressed up against him and he could feel every soft, enticing curve? He liked to think he had a hell of a lot of self-control, but he was only human.

And she was the kind of woman who could haunt a man's dreams and make him want things he shouldn't.

With no effort whatsoever, he could imagine himself sleeping with her every night for the rest of his life, building a home with her, having babies with her, growing old with her. She had a softness to her, a femininity that was incredibly appealing. Every instinct he had told him she would be the kind of lover that would turn a man inside out...

In the deepening shadows of his bedroom, he stiffened at the thought. What the devil was he doing? Priscilla had RELATIONSHIP, and, worse yet, COMMITMENT, stamped all over her, and he wasn't going there. Not again.

Jennifer, too, had appeared to be the kind of woman a man could trust to keep a commitment. She'd claimed she wanted marriage, a life with him, babies, but that was only as long as there were still stars in her eyes. When things got real, not to mention tough, commitment didn't mean a damn thing. She'd still walked out on him during the biggest crisis of his life.

Which was why there was no woman in his life now, he reminded himself. And he didn't think there ever would be. After all, he had it made playing the field. When he wanted sex, he could get it. A date for dinner was only a phone call away. And when he wanted space, he had all that he wanted. He was footloose and fancy free and didn't answer to anyone but himself. That was just the way he liked it.

So what was he still doing there, lying in bed with a woman who made him think of things he didn't want? He was only asking for trouble, and he'd had more than enough of that already just trying to keep her safe. Getting romantically involved with her could only lead to disaster.

Knowing that didn't make it any easier for him to let her go. Irritated with himself, he slowly released her and eased out of the bed, half expecting her to wake any second. But she was still dead to the world and only sighed in her sleep. Not sure if he was relieved or disappointed, he soundlessly strode across the room in his stocking feet and shut the door behind him before heading down the hall to his office, which he'd set up in the spare bedroom.

The second he shut his office door behind him, he called Buck. It wasn't until Buck growled, "This better be damn good," that he realized it was the middle of the night. With the time changes and nonstop traveling, he'd completely lost track of time.

"Damn," he muttered. "I'm sorry. I didn't even think to look at my watch—"

"Donovan? Is that you?"

"Yeah. I just wanted to let you know Priscilla and I finally made it out of England and back to the States."

"Thank God! Where are you?"

"At my place in San Diego, but we'll be leaving here as soon as she catches up on her sleep. It's too dangerous, staying in one place for long. How are things going at the ranch?"

"It's a living nightmare," Buck said flatly. "Whatever you do, don't bring Priscilla home. The ranch has been under attack ever since she was kidnapped, and it's only getting worse. Yesterday, Hunter was shot in the arm when he and Katherine went to town for groceries, and someone tried to kidnap her."

"What?!"

"They were both damn lucky," he said. "If Hunter hadn't turned unexpectedly to say something to Katherine when he was putting the groceries in the Jeep, he would have been shot in the heart."

Donovan swore softly. "Someone tried to kill him right in the middle of town? What happened? Did the police catch the bastard?"

Buck laughed, without humor. "Yeah, right. One thing you need to know is you can't depend on the authorities for anything. Oh, they try," he added, "but they're not exactly swift if you get my drift, and whoever's orchestrating all of this is damn clever. He's left very few clues, and no one ever seems to see anything."

"Are you saying no one saw a shooting right in the middle of town? At the grocery store? C'mon, Buck, someone must have seen *something!* There was a jackass walking around with a gun! What about your sister? Didn't she see the shooter?"

"She was talking to Hunter, and the shot came from behind her. And the second the shooting started, Hunter pulled her into the Jeep with him and drove to the hospital. She didn't see anything except the other customers in the parking lot running for cover."

"And the police don't have a clue who the shooter is?"

"If they do, they're not talking," he retorted. "Someone at the grocery store claims they saw a black pickup race down the alley behind the grocery store, but the windows were dark and they couldn't see the driver. And the truck had no license plates," he added in disgust. "Do you know how many black pickups there are just in this county alone? And we don't even know if this particular truck is even from around here. Without a license number or vehicle identification number, there's no way to track it down."

"After that, I imagine no one's going to town anytime soon," Donovan said dryly.

"Not unless it's an emergency," Buck said. "We're all hunkering down here and battening down the hatches. From now on, until this nightmare is over, we're having whatever groceries we need delivered. I've already made arrangements with the grocer."

"Be careful," Donovan warned. "Once the word gets out about that, someone could ambush you."

"I've already talked to the sheriff and convinced him to escort the grocer out here."

"How'd you manage to do that?" he asked. "I would have thought he'd have told you to hire a private security company."

"He did," Buck replied, "but I put his feet to the fire and reminded him that the only reason we were in danger was because he was doing such a sorry job. And it's an election year. If he wants to keep his job, he'd better step up to the plate and do the right thing, or he's going to be bombarded with a hell of a lot of bad press."

Surprised, Donovan said, "Obviously, you're not afraid of ticking off the sheriff."

"If he's not going to do his job, then we're on our own and have to do whatever's necessary to keep ourselves safe."

Donovan couldn't argue with that. "I'd do the same thing if I were in your shoes. Hell, I guess I *am* in your shoes. Keeping your sister safe isn't always easy."

"Where will you go from there?"

"I don't know." He sighed. "Obviously, anywhere but Colorado—unless, of course, you need her at the ranch."

"Not unless whoever's after the Broken Arrow finds

a way to kidnap me and Elizabeth and Katherine. If that happens, you're going to have to get Cilla home damn fast."

"You have my cell phone number," Donovan told him. "Call me if there's a problem, and we'll head for Colorado. And I'll keep in touch, of course. If we run into any problems, I'll call you immediately."

"Fair enough," he said gruffly. "Take good care of my sister."

Assuring him he would, Donovan hung up, his thoughts already jumping ahead to his next plan of action. As much as he would have liked to hole up in his apartment with Priscilla and ride out the next few weeks until the ranch was safely in the Wyatts' name, he knew that was out of the question. If whoever was after the Broken Arrow discovered that Buck had hired him to keep Priscilla safe, it would only be a matter of time before they discovered who he was and where he lived. His phone number was unlisted—his property taxes weren't even in his name—but anyone could find anyone if they knew where to look. He was going to make damn sure no one found Priscilla.

They would leave at dawn, he decided. While she was sleeping, he'd map out their strategy, collect everything they would need, then load his truck. Somewhere down the road, he knew they would have to switch vehicles again, just to make sure they couldn't be tracked; but for now, at least, the truck was the best bet. Since he had a camper on the back of his pickup, they could avoid motels and camp in national and state forests. If they were lucky, Priscilla's kidnappers wouldn't have a clue where they were until the deadline was past and the Broken Arrow was in the hands of the Wyatts for good.

Leaving Priscilla sleeping in his bedroom, he went outside to check his camper, only to discover that the battery had gone dead on his truck while he was in London. Not surprised, he hooked it up to the charger, then checked the supplies inside the camper. He normally kept it packed with canned goods, towels and clean sheets, not to mention several changes of clothes, but the temperatures in the mountains would be cool, so they would need extra blankets.

Get real, a voice in his head drawled. *There's only one bed—you're not going to get cold.*

Too late, he realized just how flawed his plan was. He'd already slept with Priscilla in his arms. If he shared a bed with her again, he wasn't going to be able to stop himself from making love to her. And that could only be a mistake. Sharing the camper—and its one bed—was out. They'd have to get a hotel room.

But that wouldn't be nearly as safe as camping in the middle of a national forest where it would be impossible to trace them, he thought. Damn! There had to be a way he could keep the woman safe without going quietly out of his mind from wanting her!

The thought nagged at him for hours, but he still didn't have any answers when he soundlessly opened the door to his bedroom right before dawn and found Priscilla exactly where he'd left her—in his bed like Sleeping Beauty. And all he wanted to do was kiss her awake.

He should have turned around right then and there and left her to wake up on her own. But he couldn't. With a will of their own, his feet led him straight to her.

Chapter 7

"C'mon, Princess, time to rise and shine. We've got to hit the road."

Lost in a dreamless sleep, Priscilla stirred slightly at the sound of the unintelligible male voice that called to her from a distant, shadowy world. Her eyes fluttered, and for a fleeting moment, she tried to swim to consciousness, but then she groggily realized she was dreaming. With an inaudible sigh, she sank back into the warm, intoxicating depths of slumber.

Before she was completely lost to the world, however, the voice was back, nagging her again, refusing to be ignored. "I'm serious," her tormentor said. "I know you're exhausted, but you can't lie around in bed all day. The truck's all packed. It's time to go."

Confused, she frowned in her sleep. *Go? Go where?*

She'd been running for her life for what seemed like a week. She wasn't going anywhere. "No," she mumbled. "Go away."

"Not without you, sweetheart."

The cocky, masculine drawl cleared the last of the sleep from her head as nothing else could. Hugging her pillow to her, she rolled over and opened her eyes a crack to find Donovan grinning at her from the bedroom doorway. "Are you always a pest, or do I just bring out the worst in you?"

Far from offended, he only laughed. "Me? A pest? You must be joking. Everyone knows I'm a sweetheart."

"Uh-huh," she said dryly, "and I'm Snow White."

"No, you're Sleeping Beauty. And you know what happened to her."

Confused, she frowned. "The wicked witch got her?"

"No, silly. The prince kissed her until she woke up."

"Oh, no!" she said quickly. "Don't even think about going there, mister. You're no Prince Charming."

She knew the second the words were out of her mouth that she'd made a mistake. He wasn't the kind of man that ignored a challenge. His blue eyes gleaming with purpose, he started toward her like a jungle cat on the prowl, stirring need in her before he ever got close enough to touch her.

Scrambling up on the bed, the pillow clutched to her breast with one hand and the other held out to stop him, she gasped, "I didn't mean it! You're right. We have to go."

"Too late." He chuckled, and reached for her. A heartbeat later, she was in his arms.

An instant before his mouth covered hers, she saw

roguish sparks dancing in his eyes. Then he was ravishing her with a playful kiss that was nothing like a kiss in a fairy tale. Laughter bubbling up inside her, she gasped, "That is *not* the way you kiss a princess!"

"Oh, really?" he growled, and tugged the pillow away from her to toss it across the room. "And what makes you an expert on how a prince kisses a princess?"

"I'm a princess, silly! Even without my crown, you should know that."

"I beg your pardon, your highness," he teased. "I'll try to do better."

His lips brushed hers ever so softly with a sensuous promise of heat…passion…need. And just that easily, he made her ache. Her smile faded, as did his. And when he pulled back just far enough to see her eyes, *she* was the one who reached for him. "Donovan…please…"

He could resist a lot of things, but not, he discovered, Priscilla Wyatt when she looked at him with eyes dark with need and said please. With a groan, he kissed her and completely forgot that he'd only been teasing when he'd threatened to kiss her if she didn't get out of bed. Then she kissed him back, and he forgot his own name.

Later, he couldn't have said how long he kissed her. It could have been seconds…hours. Days wouldn't have been enough.

Stunned by the thought, he abruptly came to his senses, but even as he pulled back, he knew he was in serious trouble. And he didn't have a clue what he was going to do about it—except put some distance between them immediately.

"We need to get going," he said hoarsely, jumping

up from the bed like she'd lit a fire under him. "I've already got the truck packed. While you get ready, I'll make some coffee to take with us."

Donovan had never run from a woman in his life, but he did then, and it was all Buck's fault. His sister was downright dangerous. Without even trying, she turned him inside out. And he couldn't take her home for weeks, he thought in frustration. Did Buck have a clue what he was asking of him?

Shaken, Priscilla stared at her reflection in the bathroom mirror and winced. She looked like a woman who had just been thoroughly kissed, and she could still see the need darkening her eyes. If Donovan hadn't stopped when he had…

Her heart thundering at the thought, she told herself she couldn't keep doing this. She couldn't keep kissing him, sharing a bed with him, dreaming about him. He'd been hired to save her from her kidnappers and protect her until she could go home again—nothing more. He wasn't her boyfriend, her lover, even a friend. She knew nothing about him except that he tracked down the scum of the earth and brought them back to justice…and that he could melt her bones with just a kiss.

What if he had a wife and a couple of kids stashed away somewhere? her common sense pointed out. Her sister Katherine had a two-year relationship with a man who had a wife and child in Paris, and she'd never suspected a thing. She was devastated when she discovered the truth, and with good reason. She was in love with Nigel and had planned to spend the rest of her life with him.

Was Donovan another Nigel? He, himself, had said that he had homes in Brazil and London and San Diego. Did he have a woman in every port? Was he that kind of man?

When every instinct she had rejected the idea, she told herself that it didn't matter anyway. She wasn't looking for a man. The only thing she was interested in was starting her career in fashion design as soon as she finished her internship with Jean Pierre. No man was interfering with that. Her mother had loved her father dearly, but her one regret was that she'd given up her budding career in design when she'd met Andrew Wyatt and fallen in love with him. Because of that, she'd urged all her children to go after their dreams. And that was exactly what Priscilla intended to do.

No more kissing, she told herself firmly as she washed her face, then brushed her teeth and hair. No more touching, no more sharing a bed with the man. Their race halfway across the world wasn't a romantic adventure. He was her hired protector—nothing more. As long as she remembered that, she'd be fine.

Holding onto her resolve, she headed for the kitchen. "Okay, I'm ready," she said coolly. "How's the coffee?"

"Strong," he retorted. "I figured we could both use it, but if you want cream—"

A sudden sharp knock at the door echoed through the apartment, surprising them both. Her stomach dropping, Priscilla whirled and looked at him with wild eyes. "Who—"

Silently holding an index finger to his mouth, he soundlessly stepped over to the door and looked through the peephole. The last thing he expected to see was a Federal Express deliveryman standing on the other side of the door.

There'd been a time when he was much younger when he would have automatically unlocked the door and opened it without a second thought. Over the years, however, he'd learned the hard way to be a hell of a lot more cautious.

"Who's there?" he grumbled through the door.

"Federal Express," the visitor replied. "I've got a delivery for you that has to be signed for."

Alarm bells clanged in Donovan's head. He hadn't been in the country in three months, and he certainly hadn't ordered anything. All his mail was being sent to England, for the moment, but he had no intention of telling that to the imposter at his door. "Just a minute," he called through the door. "I'm not dressed."

"I haven't got all day," the man retorted. "I've got other packages to deliver."

"Twenty seconds," he replied. "I'll be right back."

Whirling, he grabbed his car keys and wallet from the small table in the entryway, then took Priscilla by the arm and rushed her into his bedroom. "C'mon," he told her, throwing open the bedroom window. "We're getting out of here."

Alarmed, she paled. "Who—"

Their visitor pounded on the door so fiercely that he nearly broke it open with his fist alone. "Open up!"

"Damn!" Donovan cursed. Putting a hand on the top of Priscilla's head so she wouldn't hit it on the window, he pushed her out on the fire escape landing and followed her out. "C'mon!"

Grabbing her hand, he towed her after him, but they

were only down three steps when they heard a shout
from Donovan's apartment. A split second later, the
door was kicked in.

Donovan didn't wait to hear more. "Run!" he
shouted and pulled her down the stairs two at a time.

Less than ten seconds later, they reached the
ground...just as the "deliveryman" upstairs in
Donovan's apartment found the open window in the
bedroom. Swearing, he struggled through the window
out onto the landing. "Stop!" he cried.

It wasn't until a bullet missed Priscilla's head by
inches that they realized he had a gun.

Screaming, she never saw Donovan draw his own
gun and fire back. Suddenly, it seemed like a hail of
bullets was coming down on them and there was
nowhere to run—until Donovan jerked her around the
corner of the building.

"Get in the truck," he shouted. "Now!"

Terrified, she jerked open the passenger door and
tumbled inside just as he threw himself into the driver's
seat. He hadn't even shoved the key in the ignition
when a bullet shattered the window in the back door
of the camper on the back of Donovan's truck.

"Son of a bitch!" he cursed. "Get down!"

Not waiting to see if she obeyed, he grabbed her by
the back of the neck and pushed her head down to her
knees. Her heart slamming against her ribs, Priscilla
didn't offer a word of protest.

Later, she couldn't have said how long she hugged
her knees. Donovan hit the accelerator, sending them
shooting out of the apartment complex driveway like
a drunk on a mad tear. Horns honked sharply, and over

the squeal of brakes, Priscilla heard cursing, but she didn't dare lift her head. Not yet. Not until it was safe.

Then it hit her. They might have left their attacker behind, but they were far from safe. Whoever had just tried to kill them had not only a description of Donovan's pickup and camper but also the truck's license plate number. Anyone who had the connections to do a search of the Department of Motor Vehicles records could discover Donovan's name, pretend to be him and call to report the vehicle stolen. Every cop in the state of California would be looking for them within the hour.

"Oh, God!"

"What?" Donovan demanded, never taking his eyes from the road as he whipped through the traffic. "What's wrong?"

"There's nowhere to hide," she said hoarsely as she cautiously sat up. "They know what kind of vehicle we're in."

"Don't worry," he assured her. "We're ditching this the first chance we get."

That did little to reassure her. Suddenly more afraid than she'd ever been in her life, she found herself fighting tears. "What good will it do? They'll just find us anyway."

Frowning, he shot her a sharp look. "Hey, don't be that way. We're making progress. I got you out of England, didn't I?"

"Yes, and I appreciate it," she sniffed, "but we're not any safer here than we were in London. Look—we haven't even been here twenty-four hours and they've already found us. And we don't even know how. They couldn't have followed us all the way from England, could they?"

"No way in hell," he retorted.

"Then how…"

"I've been asking myself the same question," he said, grimacing. "It makes no sense. Whoever's after the ranch can't possibly have enough power to watch every single flight out of England or into the United States. So how could they have found us? No one even knew where we were except Buck."

"And he wouldn't have told anyone except the family."

"I've got my share of enemies," he said, "but most of them are locked up. And the ones who aren't wouldn't have knocked on the door—they'd have busted it down and burst in with guns blazing before we even knew they were here. No, this wasn't about me," he continued with a frown. "What I can't figure out is how anyone even knew we were here. I've been gone for months, and suddenly, the day I come home, some yo-yo shows up with a gun. What are the odds? It's not like Buck took out an ad and told the world he'd hired me. No one knew except the two of us."

The truth hit him then like a slap in the face. "Damn!"

Priscilla paled. "You've thought of something."

He nodded. "The only explanation that makes sense is Buck's phone is tapped."

"What?! It can't be."

"Think about it," he said. "We escape from your kidnappers, go halfway around the world and within twenty-four hours, someone tries to kill you. They didn't follow you. They don't know me, but they show up at my apartment."

"And Buck is the one who hired you and the only one you told where we are," she added. Hearing her own words, she paled as the pieces of the puzzle fell into place. "Oh, God, you're right!" she told him, stricken. "There's no other way anyone else could have known we were here. And Buck doesn't have a clue! We've got to warn him, but how can we call him? Whoever's tapping the phone will know that we're on to them."

"Good," he responded, reaching for his phone. "The bastard needs to know he's not going to get away with this garbage. And Buck needs to know that he can't say anything on the phone that he doesn't want whoever's after the ranch to know."

Quickly punching in the number, he waited impatiently for the call to go through. If he got Buck's damn voice mail—

"Hello?"

"Buck? Thank God! We were attacked at my apartment—"

"What?!"

"Priscilla's fine," he assured him quickly, "but I think your cell phone's being tapped."

"*What?*"

"It's the only explanation. No one knew where we were until I called you."

Buck swore roundly. "I don't know why I'm surprised. They've done everything else. This is just one more thing to break us."

"There can't be any further contact between us unless there's a serious emergency and Priscilla has to be there," Donovan said urgently. "If that happens, whoever's listening in on this conversation needs to know that I'll move heaven and hell to make sure Priscilla gets there so you don't lose the ranch."

"We owe you," Buck told him. "Keep her safe, and we'll see you at the end of the month."

When he hung up, Donovan tossed the phone into the console. If they were lucky, they wouldn't need to use it again until the Broken Arrow belonged to the Wyatts.

"Now what?" Priscilla asked quietly.

His mouth compressed into a flat line of determination. "We're on our own."

Something in his tone had dread pooling in the pit of her stomach. "Why don't I like the sound of that?"

His expression grave, he said, "Whoever is the mastermind behind the attacks on the ranch and your family has a hell of a lot of power. And now that he knows who I am and where I live, it won't take him long to shut me down."

"Shut you down? How? He can't do anything to you if he can't catch you."

"Sure he can," he said. "If he's as smart as he appears to be, it won't be long before he knows everything about me...credit card numbers, bank accounts, everything. All he has to do is put a freeze on everything and wait for us to run out of money. Then we'll be dead in the water."

The dread in her stomach turned over, nauseating her. "You think he has that kind of power?"

"Yes."

"But didn't Buck give you some money?"

"It's getting damn thin. I had to use most of it to get from England to here."

Priscilla had been afraid before but not like she was

now. And that infuriated her. "Who is this monster? How can he do all these things and no one know who he is?"

"Oh, someone knows," he assured her. "They're just not coming forward."

"Why? What he's doing is criminal!"

"The bad guys don't always get punished, sweetheart. From what Buck told me about Hilda Wyatt's will, a hell of a lot of people in Willow Bend seem to think they're the unnamed heir." His steel-blue gaze hardened. "So no one has a vested interest in protecting you or your family…or stopping anyone who wants to terrorize you into leaving the ranch. By standing back and doing nothing, they could end up with the ranch."

"That'll never happen," she vowed coldly. "We'll fight them every step of the way, and when this is all over and the ranch is ours, everyone involved in this damn conspiracy is going to pay for what they've done."

"They will if I have anything to do with it," he promised her, "but if they manage to shut down the credit cards, we've got to have jobs lined up."

"*Jobs?!* How can we? We'll have to stay in one place—"

"Not necessarily, but we can work out the details when we know a little bit more about the money situation." Pulling into the parking lot of his bank, he parked and cut the motor. "And we're about to find out what that is right now. C'mon."

Ten minutes later, when they walked out of the bank with five thousand dollars in cash, Donovan knew they were damn lucky. He didn't doubt that before the day was over, his credit cards, checking account and God knew what else would be shut down. From now on, they'd have to live by their wits.

"Now we've got to get rid of the truck," he said as they climbed back into the truck and headed north. "But first we have to make sure we're not being followed. Hang on."

Priscilla soon discovered that he meant that literally. With no more warning than that, he took a sharp right at the next corner, then an immediate left, then another right. If she hadn't grabbed onto the door, she would have been thrown out of her seat. Then three blocks later, he made a quick U-turn right in front of a speeding dump truck.

"Oh, God!"

"It's okay," Donovan reassured her. "I've got plenty of time."

Priscilla wasn't so sure of that. She would have sworn she felt the heat of the dump truck kiss the back bumper of the pickup as Donovan completed the U-turn. "If you get me killed, I'll never forgive you."

"Wah," he mocked. "What a baby. Think of the stories you'll be able to tell your grandchildren."

"If I live to have any," she said dryly.

"You'll die in your bed at ninety-six, surrounded by your children, grandchildren and great-grandchildren. You're that kind of woman."

Surprised, she studied him consideringly. "What does that mean?"

"You're the marrying kind," he said simply. "The kind who wants the whole nine yards—the husband, kids, the white picket fence and the minivan."

She was, but that particular dream wasn't something

she allowed herself to think about. Not yet, not until her career was off the ground. So how had he known?

"It's in your eyes," he said, reading her mind. Turning his attention back to his driving, he said, "Bingo—just what I was looking for," and shot across three lanes of traffic to a car dealership on the opposite side of the street.

The sign on the front of the building boasted that Tom Lincoln Ford bought and sold cars, trucks and RVs, and Priscilla didn't doubt it. She'd never seen so many vehicles on a car lot in her life.

"I need to sell my truck," Donovan told the salesman who came forward to greet them. "Who do we need to talk to?"

"I can take care of that for you," the man said easily. "Let me call the service manager and have it checked out. Then I'll run some numbers and see what kind of price we can come up with. Did you just want to sell it or trade it in on something else? We're having a great sale right now."

"No, we can't afford anything else right now," Donovan replied. "I've been sick lately and lost my job. If we don't get some money today, we're going to lose our house."

"Oh, man, I'm sorry to hear that," the salesman said sincerely. "Let me see what I can do."

Priscilla couldn't believe Donovan's audacity. He was telling tales to a salesman who not only heard his fair share of bad luck stories on a daily basis but, no doubt, told a few whoppers of his own. "You've been sick lately?" she asked with a delicately arched brow as soon as the salesman excused himself to work on a bid for them. "You do know that you don't look like you've missed a day of work in your life, don't you?"

He only grinned. "Hey, whatever helps the cause. I figured that was a better story than the truth. And who knows? It may work."

Priscilla doubted it, but she was willing to be proven wrong. And she didn't have long to wait. Less than fifteen minutes later, the salesman found them in the waiting area. "Okay," he said cheerfully, "everything checked out with service. Now it's just a question of making the deal. You do realize that we can only offer you wholesale?"

"Yes, of course," Donovan said. "You've got to make a profit, too."

"Exactly. And we do have to discount for wear and tear—"

"We understand how the business works," Donovan said wryly. "Just give us a figure."

The salesman gave them each a printed estimate of the value of the truck, which was based on everything from the extras on the truck and camper to the negative condition of the tires and the quarter-size dot of rust on the rear bumper. And the offer was fifteen hundred dollars *more* than Donovan had expected.

"I wish we could go higher," the salesman said, "but this is the best we can do. And the offer's good for three days if you want to think about it—"

"No, that's okay," Donovan assured him. "We'll take it."

Aware of the salesman listening to every word, Priscilla pulled him aside, "Are you sure you want to do this? There must be another way—"

Slipping his arm around her waist, Donovan turned to the salesman with a rueful smile. "Isn't she the greatest? We're losing our home and she's worried about me. It's all right, sweetheart," he assured her. "I haven't been camping in a year and a half. I can get another camper when our finances improve. Right now, this is the right move."

Just that easily, the decision was made. Without blinking an eye, he sold his pickup and camper for her.

Chapter 8

Even though Donovan had told the salesman they couldn't afford to buy a car at this time, Priscilla hadn't really believed him. But as they walked out of the dealership with the check in hand, he didn't even glance at the other cars on the lot. Surprised, she said, "Now what?"

"We walk," he replied.

"*Walk?* But—"

"Not here, sweetheart," he said as her startled exclamation drew the eye of several other customers on the lot. "C'mon. Let's get out of here."

Hurrying to keep pace with him, she frowned. "And where, exactly, are we going? Wherever it is, we're not going to get there very fast if we have to walk."

"You'd be surprised," he said with a grin, and paused at a bus stop just as a bus braked to a halt at the curb to let off some passengers. His blue eyes twinkling, he motioned for her to precede him. "Ladies first."

"You don't even know where it's going!"

Unperturbed, he chuckled. "Doesn't matter. We've got no particular destination in mind."

She knew he spoke nothing less than the truth. Maybe letting the whims of fate decide where they went was safer than having a plan. But for a woman who'd always been the kind to map things out, flitting around the world like a tumbleweed being pushed around by the wind was more than a little unsettling.

Donovan paid the fare for both of them, and they found seats near the front. When the bus headed across town, Donovan looked like he didn't have a care in the world, but Priscilla wasn't fooled. His eyes missed nothing. He might not know where they were going until they got there, but he was ready for whatever surprises popped up along the way. Reassured, she relaxed and waited for his next move.

She didn't have to wait long. Fifteen minutes later, he nudged her. "This is where we get off," he said quietly, rising to his feet.

What had he seen that she hadn't? Stepping off the bus, she looked around. There was a grocery store across the street and several strip malls farther down the road that had stores that sold everything from musical instruments to computers. Confused, she turned to him and said dryly, "I think I can safely assume you're not going to buy a saxophone or a computer, so we must be going to the grocery store."

"Nope," he said as he took her hand. "C'mon."

When he started back the way they had come, she

stopped in her tracks. "We just came this way on the bus. Why are we going back?"

"Ye of little faith," he teased. "I thought you trusted me."

If he hadn't had a twinkle in his eye, she might have. "I do," she said. "Sometimes."

He only laughed. "Well, that's a start, anyway. Look down the street, sweetheart, and tell me where we're going."

Walking at his side, her hand still in his, she studied the businesses lining the street for at least a mile in the distance. Signs of varying size and height littered the airspace, vying for attention and making it almost impossible to read any individual sign. Then the tallest one caught her attention, and she wondered why she hadn't guessed sooner.

"You're buying a car."

"Yeah. So what's so funny?" he asked when he saw her lips twitch into a half smile.

"I'm learning how your mind works. That's a scary thought."

He lifted a dark brow at her. "Really, Miss Smarty Pants. So tell me what I'm thinking."

"You didn't buy a car at the dealership where you sold your truck because you were covering your bases in case my kidnappers find a way to trace the sale. This way, they won't know what kind of car we're switching to."

"Smart girl," he said, pleased. "Never broadcast your personal business. The less you tell people, the less they can repeat. If your kidnappers do find the camper, the only thing the dealership can tell them is that we walked away."

"For all they know, we could have had a taxi waiting around the corner," she pointed out.

"True," he agreed. "If I were tracking us, I'd call all the taxi services in town to see if any of their drivers picked up a couple anywhere near Tom Lincoln Ford. If they didn't, I'd check out the transit system."

"That could take a while," she said. "You have to discover the closest bus stops to Tom Lincoln Ford, then check out all the routes the buses run from this area." She sighed. "In a city the size of San Diego, how many people does a bus driver see in a day? How can he possibly remember a man and woman who quietly ride the bus and do nothing to draw attention to themselves?"

"He doesn't have to," he replied, "if the buses have video cameras in them."

Surprised, she felt her heart sink. "Do they?"

"You didn't notice?"

She had to admit she hadn't. "Did you?"

He nodded. "There was a camera. It looked like it was out of commission, but we can't count on that."

"So that's why you didn't take the stop by the dealership," she said, understanding. "They may eventually discover which stop we got off at, but they won't know where we went from there."

"And even if they make their way back to the dealership, they'll never know we were there because we're going to come in separately and leave the same way. I'll pick you up down the street, and no one will even suspect we were together. Okay?"

It was a good plan, one she had no complaints with...except when they split up. Her common sense told her nothing was going to happen at the dealership, and if it did, Donovan would be within screaming distance if she needed him. There was nothing to worry about. So why was her heart racing just at the thought of walking away from him? What was wrong with her?

"Hello?" When she looked up at him and blinked, he smiled crookedly. "Where did I lose you?"

Heat burned her cheeks. "Sorry," she said with a grimace. "I heard you. I was just thinking."

"About what?"

You. The single word almost popped out before she could stop it. Had she lost her mind? she wondered. One slip of the tongue and he would take that and run with it. She didn't even want to think about how he would tease her.

"Actually," she murmured, "I was wondering how we're going to do this. If you don't mind, I'll go in first and get one of the salesmen to show me around while you find a car. Then when it looks like you're about to leave, I'll make an excuse to my salesman and leave. You can pick me up around the corner."

He smirked. "You're getting pretty damn good at this. Who knows? By the time this is all over with, we could go into business together."

"Not unless you're going to model my designs," she retorted. "That would certainly earn some looks in the industry, but that wasn't exactly the market I was striving for."

He ran a teasing finger down her nose. "Brat. One of these days, you're going to pay for all that sass."

Not the least intimidated by the threat, she only

grinned. "One can only hope. Now, if you'll excuse me, I have to go find a salesman."

An hour later, Priscilla was running out of questions to ask Kevin Richards, the salesman who'd approached her the moment she'd walked onto the car lot. What she knew about cars could fit in a thimble, and it was obvious. To his credit, though, Kevin Richards was being incredibly patient. Not once did he roll his eyes whenever she asked something a first grader should have known.

Searching her brain for something else to ask, she suddenly saw Donovan step out of the dealership office and shake hands with a salesman who smiled and handed him a set of keys. That was her cue to leave.

"You've been very kind," she told Kevin, "and I feel really awful that I've taken up so much of your time. But I really don't see anything my husband would like."

"But this is Motor Trend's truck of the year," he said, frowning. "I'm sure your husband would love it. Why don't you call him and see if he can come in? I'd be happy to talk to him."

"Oh, he doesn't like to deal with salesmen," she said quickly, smiling like a woman whose only goal in life was to make her man's life easier. "That's why he has me. I'll talk to him, though," she promised, "and tell him about the Ford. If he's interested, I'll come back and see what kind of price you can give us."

From his quick scowl, Kevin obviously didn't like that suggestion at all, but he managed to hang on to his temper. "It would be better if your husband would come in himself, but if he won't, I guess there's not much we can do about it." Reaching into his coat pocket, he handed her his card. "I work Tuesday through Sunday. If your husband decides he wants to see one of the trucks, I'll talk to my manager about driving it over to your house."

"That's a great idea! I'll be in touch."

He'd already walked away, and with a sigh of relief, she left the dealership behind and started walking down the street. Cars whizzed past, and for an instant, from out of nowhere, fear spiraled through her. She was so close to the street, she thought, shaken. Anyone driving by could snatch her into a car without even slowing down.

Where was Donovan? Was he already in their pre-arranged spot? What if she missed him? What if—

Suddenly realizing what she was doing, she stiffened. She had to stop this! Donovan wouldn't miss her or, for that matter, let anything happen to her. Right now, he was probably watching her every move. If she needed him, he'd be there for her in a matter of seconds.

The pounding of her heart eased just at the thought that he was nearby. Later, she knew she would have to deal with the knowledge that he made her feel safe in a way that no man ever had; but for the moment, she had other things to worry about…like meeting Donovan at the appointed spot. Picking up her pace, she turned right at the next corner.

Donovan was nowhere in sight.

Her heart sank. "Oh, no!"

"Need a ride, lady?"

Startled, she whirled to her right to discover

Donovan parked in a bay of a self-serve car wash. Parked in full view of the street, but not the least bit noticeable, the dark-green Chevy he'd bought didn't draw a single glance from the occasional driver who turned down the side street.

"Thank God!" she said in relief. "You scared me to death! I thought you'd be parked at the curb waiting for me."

"This was safer," he told her as she hurried over to the car and slipped into the passenger seat. "Did you have any problems?"

"No, I just felt so exposed. Do you think anyone at the car lot suspected we were together?"

"Not at all. I don't know what story you told that salesman, but whatever it was, he looked completely frustrated with you."

She grinned. "I pretended I was looking at trucks for my husband. Of course, I don't know a thing about trucks, and it was obvious. He never lost his patience, but he was so frustrated, he wanted to pull his hair out. When I saw you were about to leave, I told him I couldn't buy anything without talking to my husband first. He couldn't get rid of me fast enough," she said.

"Good," he said, pleased. "If your kidnappers do find a way to trace us, all your salesman will be able to tell them is a married lady came in to look at trucks for her husband. He didn't see where you came from or where you went."

"Thank God!" she said. "So where do we go from here?"

"Los Angeles," he said promptly, heading north. "It's a good place to get lost in."

Relieved—and feeling safe for the first time in what seemed like months—Priscilla leaned back in her seat and watched as he maneuvered through the traffic with the skill of a race car driver. She knew Los Angeles was straight up the interstate from San Diego, but when Donovan didn't even take the interstate, she wasn't really surprised. If there was one thing she'd learned over the course of the last few days, it was that he very seldom did the expected.

Curious, she asked, "How did you become a bounty hunter and learn to track bad guys? That's not a line of work many people go into. How did you learn all the tricks of the trade?"

He grinned. "Are you asking if I learned from personal experience?"

Startled, she blushed. "I didn't mean—"

"I was a cop, sweetheart. I learned just about everything I needed to know from the scum I arrested on the streets."

"And now you work for yourself? Why? I don't know how much you make, but I would think that you'd make more—and have a heck of a lot more benefits— if you worked for the police department. Not that it's any of my business," she added quickly. "I'm not trying to be nosy or anything. I'm just curious."

Donovan hesitated. He didn't normally talk about his past, but they were going to be spending weeks together before she could go home. She had a right to know who she was on the run with.

"I never had much use for rules—"

A grin kicked up one corner of her mouth. "No kidding? Tell me something I don't know."

"Smart ass," he said and chuckled. "Do you want to hear this or not?"

"Sorry," she said, fighting a smile. "Proceed, please."

"As I was saying before I was so rudely interrupted," he drawled, "I never had much use for rules, but I played by the book. My arrests were always clean. I made sure of it."

"And?"

Sobering, he said, "Johnny Sanchez was my best friend on the force. We went to high school together and joined the force the same day."

Her eyes searching his, she frowned. "Why do I have the feeling that he wasn't as ethical as you were?"

"He was on the take," he said bluntly.

"*On the take?*" Her eyes widened. "You mean he was taking bribes?"

His gaze shifting between the road ahead of them and the rearview mirror, he nodded grimly. "He wasn't the only one. Several detectives were doing the same thing."

"What did you do?"

"I was furious," he replied. "I had a meeting with Johnny and raked his butt over the coals. I warned him I was going to turn him and the others in if he didn't go to the chief."

"And did he?"

Just thinking about Johnny and his betrayal had a muscle ticking in his jaw. "No."

"So you went to the chief."

It wasn't a question, but a statement, and he appreciated the fact that she realized he was the kind of man who kept his word. Except that he hadn't had a chance to do that when it came to Johnny. "Johnny and his buddies framed me before I could do anything," he retorted. "They planted drugs in my car, then had one of their buddies on the force stop me the next morning as I was driving into work."

"Oh, my God!" she gasped. "What happened?"

"I was charged with possession and arrested." Five years had passed since then, but the memory still had the power to enrage him. "I spent a year in prison."

"Are you serious? But you were set up! Surely someone at the police station must have listened to you."

"Oh, sure," he said bitterly. "They listened, for all the good it did me. Planting evidence without leaving any prints is a piece of cake for a bunch of rogue cops. And with no evidence against them, it came down to my word against theirs. Most of them were all detectives with impeccable reputations. I followed the rules, but I'd always been a rebel and everyone knew it. I didn't have a prayer's chance in hell."

"So they just got away with it?" she said incredulously.

"No, though there were some dark nights when I was in prison when I thought they were going to." He didn't tell her about the rage that had engulfed him at those times, or the need for revenge that had come close to stealing his soul. It had taken a lot of work on his part, but he'd locked those emotions away in the deepest part of his brain, and he didn't plan to ever go there again. "I didn't know at the time that one of the other detectives on the force who was clean believed me. He worked with Johnny and his partners in crime and began secretly gathering evidence against them. When he had enough, he went to the chief without anyone knowing it, and they were all arrested."

"So you were released?"

"Only when Johnny copped a plea and finally told the truth," he muttered. "He didn't do it out of any concern for me. He was just saving his own ass."

"What a slimeball," she seethed. "He was your friend. My God, you went to school together! How could he let you just rot in prison without coming forward right from the very beginning?"

"Money," he said simply. "You'd be surprised what people will do to get their hands on it. Though I don't have to tell you that," he added. "Look what the good folks in Willow Bend are doing to you and your family to get the ranch. According to Buck, they've tried to burn you out, shoot you, kidnap you—they even put rattlesnakes in your beds!"

"They're sociopaths," she said. "They have to be to even consider doing something like that. Of course, they don't think they're ever going to get caught. After a year in prison, it can't be much consolation to you, but at least your friend Johnny and the others paid for what they did."

Donovan didn't have the heart to tell her they were already out on the streets. Johnny only got six months, and the others, three years. Justice, he thought sarcastically, was a wonderful thing.

"So is that why you didn't go back to the force?" Priscilla asked as he again took an unexpected turn to make sure they weren't being followed. "Surely, they would have taken you back."

"I didn't want to go back," he said flatly. "I moved

to Chicago and applied there, but when they did a background search and discovered I'd turned in fellow cops, no one wanted to work with me."

"That's ridiculous!" she snapped. "You were the good guy."

He smiled at her vehemence. "Why, Prissy, I didn't know you cared."

"Stuff it," she growled. "This is about right and wrong, and you did the right thing. How could anyone find fault with that?"

"There's an unwritten code—"

"Bite me," she spat out. "You were a police officer enforcing the law."

"Maybe that works in the movies and fairy tales, but not in the real world. And things turned out all right, anyway," he explained. "I went into business for myself and became a bounty hunter. I travel all over the world, I don't have to play by the rules anymore and I still get to catch the bad guys. Life doesn't get any better than that."

Another woman might have been fooled by his devil-may-care attitude, but Priscilla could still see the flash of bitterness in his eyes when he'd spoken of Johnny and the detectives who had nearly destroyed his life. She couldn't blame him for being disillusioned and cynical. Who wouldn't be?

"You don't get tired of the traveling?" she asked curiously. "Of sleeping in a different bed every other night? Of being in a strange town every time you turn around?"

He shrugged. "Sometimes. But every job has its drawbacks. It has its perks, too."

What perks? she wanted to ask. There couldn't be a

woman in his life…well, not just one special one, anyway. How could there be? His job took him all over the world, and he didn't stay anywhere very long before he moved on. What woman would put up with that?

Still, she knew there must have been one at one time. Donovan was the kind of man women were attracted to. She knew from personal observation that he couldn't walk down the street without drawing the eye of every female in sight. Surely, at least one woman must have tried to tie him down. And he must have been tempted. What happened? Why weren't they together?

Suddenly realizing where her thoughts had wandered, she stiffened. What was wrong with her? Whether or not there was a woman in Donovan's life had nothing to do with her. He was her bodyguard, hired to keep her safe until she could go home to the ranch in a few weeks. Once she no longer needed him to keep her safe, he would move on to his next job, and she'd probably never see him again.

Wasn't that what she wanted? To be free of the fear that dodged her every step, to be in charge of her life again, to be able to go anywhere she wanted alone?

The answer didn't come nearly as quickly as she would have liked. Confused, stunned by the sudden twinge in the region of her heart, she was mortified to discover that she was on the verge of tears. Blinking furiously, she glanced away and stared blindly out the window. She had to get a grip, she told herself fiercely. Whatever she was feeling for him was nothing more than a result of the fact that they were practically living in each other's pocket. Once this was all over and she could put some space between them, she'd be fine.

And if you believe that one, a voice drawled in her head, *then get your sketches ready because the Queen wants you to design a new wardrobe for her! Idiot. Get real.*

"You all right?"

Lost in her musings, she almost laughed. All right? Not hardly. "I'm fine," she lied. Suddenly realizing they'd reached the outskirts of Los Angeles while she was brooding over her thoughts, she managed. "Where do we go from here?"

"Since there's no way in hell we're going back to my apartment, we've got to get some clothes," he replied. "Then we look for work."

Finding clothes was easy enough—they stopped at a second-hand shop and bought just about everything they needed. Finding work that Donovan approved of, however, was something else entirely. There were plenty of places advertising for help, but Donovan passed them all by for one reason or another. Then, just when Priscilla was beginning to wonder if they were going to drive all the way to San Francisco before they stopped, he found just what he was apparently looking for…a small, old-fashioned diner next door to an old travel court that looked like it had been there since the forties.

Pleased, he pulled around to the rear of the diner and parked, making sure they were out of sight of anyone driving past on the road. "This should do nicely," he told her. "These kind of places don't do background checks—or ask too many questions, for that matter. Let's go check it out."

The diner was packed…and a madhouse. Tables needed to be cleaned, customers waited impatiently for someone to take their orders and the old man working the grill looked like he was ready to pull his hair out as he shouted at the one waitress he had to pick up the orders he'd just completed and be quick about it. She only shot him a hostile look and moved at her own pace.

The situation looked far from ideal to Priscilla, but Donovan took one look at the place and grinned. "This is a sure thing if I ever saw it." Raising his voice over the din of the jukebox and customers demanding to know when their order was going to be ready, he told the old man, "You look like you could use some help, and we're looking for work."

"You found it," the old man rasped as he flipped hamburgers on the grill. "Grab an apron from the back and one of you get back here and either flip burgers or start three orders of chicken-fried steak. The other can help Janie before all my customers walk out."

"You cook," Donovan told Priscilla. "I'll wait tables."

Horrified, she said, "Oh, no. Desserts are my thing, not chicken-fried steak. I don't even know what it is."

"Your education is sadly lacking," he teased, "but we'll have to do something about that later." Handing her an apron, he grinned. "Go wait tables, sweetheart. I've got some steaks to cook."

Just that easily, they both had jobs.

Chapter 9

Priscilla had never waited tables in her life, but as she moved through the diner taking orders, cleaning tables, refilling coffee cups and iced tea glasses, she couldn't remember the last time she'd had so much fun.

Oh, she made more than a few mistakes, mixed up some orders and even dropped a bowl of chicken and dumplings, though not, thankfully, on a customer. She'd thought she was history then, but Harry Thomas, the old man who hired her and Donovan and owned the diner, only rolled his eyes and dished up another bowl of dumplings. That was hours ago, and she hadn't dropped another dish since. She was, she thought with satisfaction, getting the hang of this.

"Hey, Miss Sunshine," Donovan teased her as the last two customers left and Mr. Thomas locked the door behind them. "If I didn't know better, I'd swear you've done this before."

Pleased, she grinned. "I did all right, didn't I?"

"Except for the chicken and dumplings," Mr. Thomas said dryly. "And the plates and coffee cups you chipped when you cleaned tables. Oh, yeah, and the sugar you put in the salt shaker—"

"Hey, they were both white!" she said, when she saw the twinkle gleaming in his faded blue eyes. "I was in a hurry and forgot what was what. Thank God I didn't grab the flour by mistake."

"Good point." He chuckled. He added gruffly, "Did I say thank you? An hour before you two walked in, my cook and head waitress walked out and left me high and dry. I don't know what I would have done if you hadn't come in when you had."

"You helped us, too," Donovan said. "We both needed jobs, and you gave us a chance. We owe you."

"And I'll pay you on Friday," he assured him with a wink, "after you work all week."

"Then I guess we'll see you in the morning," Donovan said. "What time do we need to report to work?"

"Five in the morning." At their groan, he said, "Quit your whining. You're a hell of a lot younger than I am and you don't see me crying. And we open at six. You can't show up ten minutes before the first customer walks in the door and expect anything but chaos."

Suitably chastised, Donovan and Priscilla nodded. "We'll be there," they said in unison.

"Then get your butts out of here," he barked. "You've been off the clock for twenty minutes."

"What?!"

Laughing, Donovan grabbed a sputtering Priscilla and pulled her out the back door.

They only had to go across the street to get a motel room, but even though they'd had a long, busy day, Priscilla was high on success. "I can't believe that was so much fun!" she said as Donovan unlocked the door to their room. "I was so afraid I was going to bungle everything, but it was fun. You seemed to do okay in the kitchen. You must have been a line cook before. Everyone said the food was great. Even Harry seemed impressed."

"Harry was desperate," he retorted wryly as he followed her inside and locked the door behind him. "All I had to do to impress him was know how to turn on a burner. Are you tired?"

She shrugged. "Not particularly. I guess I'm too excited. I feel like I've run a marathon or something. How many chicken-fried steaks did you make today?"

He groaned at the thought. "I didn't count, but it felt like a hundred and five."

Too restless to sit still, she pulled off her shoes then jumped up to prowl around the room. "Did you notice my American accent?" she asked as he set the two small suitcases they'd bought at the second-hand shop on the chest and began to unpack his things. "I was afraid I'd get flustered and drop it, but I didn't. I just pretended I was playing a part in a play. It was great! No one even suspected I was British."

"You did very well," he told her. "I didn't know you had it in you."

"Hey!"

"Just kidding," he said. "You're a natural. You'd

make a great private investigator, you know. You think fast on your feet."

Pleased, she smiled. "Thank you. I try."

"You did more than try. You threw yourself into your part like you'd been playing it all your life. Are you sure you want to be a designer? You'd have a hell of a lot more fun chasing bad guys."

Her green eyes lit up at the compliment. "Designing has its fair share of espionage," she pointed out. "Trust me, it's not dull."

"I'm sure it's not. And you are the artsy-fartsy type. It sticks out all over you."

Her eyes narrowed dangerously. "*Artsy-fartsy?* And just what do you mean by that?"

"Now don't get all bent out of shape," he said quickly. "That was a compliment."

"Really? How do you figure that?"

"Look at you. You've been kidnapped *twice,* first by the jackasses that broke into your apartment, then by me. You've been dragged halfway around the world. You don't even have your own clothes or makeup with you so you're stuck wearing whatever you've been able to pick up along the way and throw together." He gazed at her with admiration. "Most women would not only have a fit at living that way but they'd look like they'd been Dumpster diving. But not you. You're wearing clothes from a thrift store, for God's sake, but if I didn't know better, I'd swear you spent at least a couple hundred dollars on that outfit. It looks like it was made for you, and all you did was add some scarves and funky shoes and clunky jewelry. If that's not artsy-fartsy, I don't know what is."

Touched, she smiled. "I just have an eye for putting things together."

"No, it's more than that. You've got talent, and that talent's going to make you a heck of a lot of money one of these days."

Delighted with the prediction, she beamed. "You can say you knew me when I waited tables and wore dollar jewelry."

"And when you were so tired from working all day that you were loopy," he teased. "Five o'clock comes awfully early. Don't you think you should go to bed?"

Cocking her head, she studied him coyly. "Is this another trick to sleep with me? Don't think I haven't noticed that there's only one bed in this room...or I've forgotten what happened in your apartment, Donovan. I may be loopy, but there's nothing wrong with my memory."

She was feeling full of herself and had no idea how incredibly sexy and cute she was. And if he wasn't half dead on his feet, he would have already reached for her. "Sweetheart, I can't believe I'm saying this, but you're perfectly safe. I'm a walking zombie. But if it'll make you feel better, I'll sleep on top of the covers and you can sleep between the sheets." And just to prove it, he stretched out on top of the bedspread and grinned at her tiredly. "How's that?"

Her heart pounding, she should have said no. Things had gotten entirely too heated the last time the two of them had shared a bed, and it was all his fault. He was too attractive, too sexy, too...everything! Every time he touched her, kissed her, even teased her, she found it more and more difficult to resist the need he stirred in her, and it had to stop. Now!

But he was exhausted—he could barely keep his eyes open—and now that the adrenaline that had kept her running all day had started to fade, she realized just how tired she was. Dropping down to the side of the bed, she winced as she slipped off her tight shoes. This was crazy, she told herself. What was she thinking? They were both adults, for heaven's sake, not randy teenagers who couldn't control themselves! And they had to be at work at five in the morning. If they both didn't go to sleep immediately, they were crazy.

"Feet hurt?" Donovan asked with a frown when she rubbed her foot. "We're probably both going to need better shoes."

"I never even noticed how much they were burning," she said, massaging her instep. "I think I'm getting a blister."

"Here…let me see," he said, and sat up to reach for her foot.

At his first touch, Priscilla swallowed a quick, nearly soundless gasp. She'd never known her feet were so sensitive. She should have found some excuse to pull back, but she couldn't seem to think, couldn't seem to do anything except imagine his hands moving from her feet to her ankles, up her calves to—

Lost in the magic of his touch, she sighed in pleasure, only to try to jerk free when he trailed a teasing finger down the sole of her foot. "Donovan—"

Amusement gleamed in his eyes. "Yes?"

He ran his finger down her instep again, making her laugh. "Don't!" she protested when he tickled her again.

"Don't what?" he asked innocently, chuckling as he struggled to keep her from kicking him. "I'm just giving you a foot massage!"

Squirming, unable to stop laughing, she finally jerked her foot out of his grasp, only to realize her mistake almost immediately. Lightning quick, his hands moved to her ribs and set her laughing all over again.

"Stop!" she said, grabbing his hands as laughter bubbled up inside her. "You're killing me!"

"Say uncle, and I'll think about it."

"Uncle," she gasped. "UNCLE!"

Chuckling, he rolled with her on the bed, and when they came to a stop, he was half covering her as his eyes smiled down into hers. "Wimp," he teased. "You didn't hold out thirty seconds."

"I did, too! You couldn't do half that good."

"Wanna bet?"

Snatching up the challenge, she immediately attacked his ribs, tickling him furiously. When he just grinned and lifted a brow at her, she scowled. "That's inhuman."

That was the wrong thing to say. Lying with her on the bed, the soft curve of her breasts flush against his chest, he was human, all right, and aching for her. His gaze dropped to the sweet, enticing curve of her mouth, and as he watched, her lips parted just a fraction. Swallowing a groan, he told himself this was madness—he had to let her go. But it was already too late for that. He couldn't.

And she felt the kick of the attraction between them as surely as he did—he saw the heat in her eyes, felt her sudden stillness as awareness reached out of the darkness to steal the air right out of both their lungs. "This isn't smart," she said huskily.

"Maybe not," he said, "but it feels right. If you want me to let you go, though, I will. Just say the word, but be damn quick about it. You've got two seconds."

Her eyes dark and sultry, she just looked at him.

Donovan liked to think that he was a man in charge of his emotions, but from the second he'd first laid eyes on her, he hadn't been able to stop himself from wanting her. "One," he growled. "Two—"

The word was still on his lips when he kissed her, and just that quickly, need clawed at him like a hungry beast. He wanted to touch her, kiss her...everywhere. His mouth hot and hungry on hers, he blindly reached for buttons and snaps, moaning as her naked breasts spilled into his hands. Soft. No woman had a right to be so soft, or so responsive. His thumb barely grazed her nipple, and she arched under him with a sigh of pleasure that was nearly his undoing.

"Donovan."

That was all she said, just his name, but she called to him in a way that somehow touched his soul. The need to rush faded, then disappeared completely. Transfixed, he found himself lingering, seducing, learning with his mouth and tongue and hands every secret she had.

Her senses attuned to each kiss, each whisper-soft stroke of his fingers, Priscilla reached for him. How could he know so much about her body? How could he know that when he kissed her on just the right spot on the side of her neck that her bones seemed to melt? Or that her left breast was so much more sensitive than her right? Or that she loved it when he stroked her like he couldn't stop touching her? How could he know those things?

She wanted to ask, but he trailed his hands over her again, stealing her breath, heating her blood, and her mind blurred. There was just Donovan—his lean, hard body, his hungry kisses, the sure, slow glide of his hands—and the fire he lit low in her belly.

Later, she couldn't say when or how his clothes disappeared. Suddenly, they were skin to skin, and the fire that blazed between them grew into an inferno. A sob of need rising in her throat, Priscilla thought she couldn't bear the pleasure another second when he surged into her. Then he moved. With a startled cry that was his name, she shattered.

Dawn was still a promise in the dark when Donovan woke to find Priscilla snuggled close against his back, snoring softly. Listening to her, he grinned and promised himself he was going to tease her about that later. For now, though, all he wanted to do was turn over and kiss her awake. If he did, however, he knew he wouldn't be able to stop with just a kiss. Not after the lovemaking they'd shared.

Sensual images came at him from a thousand different directions—Priscilla kissing him, moving over him, under him, coming apart in his arms. Did she know what she did to him? How she drove him crazy and made it impossible for him to think of anything but the softness of her skin, her breasts, the musky, intoxicating scent of her?

If he had any sense, he'd get out of bed and never

sleep with her again. He was slipping. He could feel the cracks in his armor and it scared the hell out of him. He could see the lingering shadows of her dreams in her eyes every time he looked at her...touched her...kissed her...made love to her. And he wanted to trust her so badly he ached with the need. But he couldn't.

So what the devil was he doing lying in bed next to her, torturing himself with the idea of making love to her again?

Before he could even begin to come up with an answer, the alarm went off, shattering his musings. Next to him, Priscilla groaned and covered her head with her pillow. "Tell me it's not time to get up."

"Sorry, Charlie," he retorted. "We've got thirty minutes to get ready before we have to report to work. Do you want the shower first or last?"

Her face still covered with her pillow, she didn't move so much as a muscle. "First, I guess," she said in a muffled voice. "How much time did you say I had?"

"*We* have thirty minutes," he retorted. "*You* have fifteen."

"But you're going to give me five of yours, aren't you?"

When she moved the pillow away from her face just enough to grin up at him, she had no idea just how tempting she was. "You think you're cute, don't you?" He chuckled. "Your extra five minutes are ticking. Move it or lose it."

Too late, he realized he probably shouldn't have given her that particular ultimatum when she was lying naked in his bed. Laughing, she threw the covers off and ran for the bathroom. Donovan took two steps after her before he realized what he was doing and abruptly stopped. He was, he thought with a muttered curse, losing his mind. If he joined her in the shower, not only would they be late to work but they might not make it at all.

Frustrated, wanting her more than he'd ever wanted a woman in his life, he told himself he had to stop this. He had to stop aching for her, reaching for her, thinking about her and how she could drive him crazy with just a touch, a kiss. But, damn, she didn't make it easy for him. He could hear her singing in the shower. *Singing,* for heaven's sake! And she was god-awful! he thought with a laugh. What was he going to do with her?

He wouldn't even let himself go there.

Harry Thomas was waiting for them when they arrived at the diner, and even though he was as gruff as ever and didn't appear to be particularly glad to see them, Priscilla saw the relief that flashed in his eyes before he quickly blinked it away. He hadn't expected them to show up, she realized. Instantly sympathetic, she didn't have to ask what he would have done if they hadn't. He'd have handled things just as he had yesterday and lost half his customers.

"What is Harry going to do when we leave?" she asked Donovan quietly as they both started preparations for not only breakfast but lunch as well. Chicken and dumplings had to be made for the lunch special, as well as the soup of the day. Using the recipe that Harry had given them, Priscilla began cleaning and chopping the vegetables while Donovan put chickens on to boil. "We need to let him know that we're not staying very long so he'll have time to hire someone before we move on. We can't just leave him high and dry."

"We can't tell anyone our plans," he said in a hushed voice that wouldn't carry to the older man, who was at the far end of the kitchen cracking eggs for omelets and breakfast burritos. "It's just too dangerous."

"But—"

"No buts, Priscilla. You have to trust me."

She did—more than ever after last night—but she couldn't just walk out on a man who had stepped forward and given them a job when they needed one. "I don't have to tell him when—"

"*I* don't even know when," he admitted. "And now that I know you're going to tell the world, I'm not going to tell you when I do know."

Undeterred, she said, "I'm not going to tell the world, silly. Just give Harry a hint."

Amused, he lifted a brow. "Really? And how do you plan to do that? Announce it during the morning rush so everyone can tell you goodbye? Or just give Harry our itinerary when we give our notice? Of course, you could send him postcards from our travels. He can post them on the diner bulletin board, and everyone can know where we've gone."

Letting him have his little joke, she merely smiled. "Just wait. My turn's coming."

"What are you two jawing about?" Harry grumbled. "Someone needs to start the coffee, then get the sausage and bacon going. We open in fifteen minutes."

"I'm on it," Priscilla volunteered. "I was just telling…" She hesitated, trying to remember the names

Donovan had used when he'd introduced her and himself to the older man yesterday. John? Joe? Joshua? "Justin!" she said quickly, suddenly remembering. "I was telling Justin that we were lucky we could go anywhere and get a job. It gives us a real sense of freedom, you know?"

His gaze narrowed slightly, but all he said was, "People move around a lot in this business. It's the nature of the beast."

"It must be difficult, keeping help," Priscilla said quietly. "People probably quit all the time without bothering to give notice."

He shrugged. "Someone else always comes along." Glancing past her to the diner's entrance, he could clearly see cars pulling into the parking lot. "Enough jawing," he barked. "The first customers are here. Time to open the doors."

They worked right through breakfast, lunch and dinner and were only able to snatch a few stolen moments for a break. For the second day in a row, Priscilla worked harder than she ever had in her life, but as she and Donovan headed for their room after they'd helped Harry close up at the end of the day, she felt the satisfaction of a job well done. It had been a good day.

"You're looking pretty damn pleased with yourself," Donovan told her as she practically danced into their room. "You made a bundle in tips, didn't you?"

She shrugged. "Don't know yet. I haven't had a chance to check yet."

"I could help you with that—"

"Oh, no!" She laughed, skipping away when he tried to grab her purse. "Count your own money."

"I don't get tips," he reminded her.

"That's not my fault. You could have waited tables."

"And you would have cooked? If I remember correctly, you're the same woman who said, *'I don't even know what chicken-fried steak is,'*" he quoted, mimicking her exactly. "How many orders for chicken fried steak do you think you've taken over the last two days? There had to be at least a couple hundred, maybe more. The way I figure it, I should get half your tips for every one of those steaks. Fifty percent of fifteen percent of two hundred steaks would be—"

"Highway robbery!" she retorted. "You're crackers!"

Making no effort to hold back a grin, he said, "How very British of you. Maybe we should start a new rule. All money goes in the till. If there's any left when this is all over, we split it fifty-fifty."

"Good idea," she replied. "I've got my contribution. Where's yours?"

Amused, he lifted a brow. "Excuse me? Have you forgotten my pickup and camper? I sold them to save your neck."

"But you bought a car. Is that half mine?"

"Of course not!"

"So what's mine is half yours but what's yours is all yours?" she challenged, fighting a smile. "Is that what you're saying?"

"Works for me," he said and chuckled. "What's wrong with that?"

Laughing, she threw a five dollar bill at him. "There's your fifty percent."

When he grinned and tucked it into his pocket, Priscilla felt her heart skip a beat. He was such a tease, and he had no idea what the wicked amusement flashing in his eyes did to her. Every time he'd looked up from the grill to smile at her, every time his husky, masculine voice reached out to stroke her as he joked with Harry or one of the customers seated at the counter, every nerve ending in her body tingled in response. What had he done to her? she wondered, shaken. She knew nothing about his past, how many women there'd been, if there was one now, and that should have bothered her. Instead, she just wanted him to kiss her again, make love to her again.

She was in big big trouble.

"You're awfully quiet all of a sudden," he said gruffly. "You all right?"

She should have said yes. She should have said anything but what popped out of her mouth. "Actually, I was wondering if you've ever been married."

He didn't so much as blink. "No."

Just no. No more, no less. Sitting back in her chair, she frowned across the table at him. "That's it? No? No, you were never even tempted? No, but you had your chances? No, you asked her but she said no? Which is it? What's your history?"

For a moment, she didn't think he was going to answer her. He hesitated, considering his words, then muttered, "No, I asked and she said yes."

That surprised her. "Then where is she?"

"I asked her before everything went south with my job. When I went to prison, she broke things off. It turns out she had an aversion to marrying a man with a prison record," he said flatly. "I can't understand why. Guess she was a snob."

"But you were framed! If she loved you, how could she not know that you were innocent? What kind of moron was she?"

"What makes you think she was wrong?"

She gave him a withering glance. "Save it," she retorted. "You're not that kind of man."

"And how do you know that?"

"Because you're not!" she snapped, stung. "Anybody with any brains knows that. You've gone above and beyond the call of duty rescuing me from my kidnappers. You didn't have to do that. You could have taken Buck's money and never really looked for me. He would have never known the difference."

"Maybe not," he acknowledged. "But I would have."

"Which is my point exactly," she said promptly. "You're an honorable man. If your fiancée didn't know that, then she didn't have any business accepting your proposal to begin with."

"She chose to believe the lies instead of the man she claimed to love. So much for happily ever after, huh?"

He hadn't trusted a woman since and didn't plan to. He didn't say the words, but she heard him loud and clear. He didn't plan to ever get mixed up with a woman again, at least not in anything that involved trust and commitment; and she couldn't blame him.

She should have been pleased. After all, the only thing she was interested in at this point in her life was finishing her internship and starting her career. Getting into design school had been tough—making the grade even tougher. It would take a hell of a lot of hard work to succeed in a business where the greats were known by one name. She wouldn't risk years of study and a dream she'd had since childhood for a man.

But there was something about Donovan, something that clicked between them every time their eyes met. And it scared the hell out of her. How could she be tempted by a man who wanted nothing to do with commitment?"

Chapter 10

Frustrated, confused, she needed some time to herself to think, to consider her options and decide what she was going to do; but that was next to impossible when they were in a motel room that was hardly bigger than the inside of a large SUV. She couldn't go for a walk or a drive without him insisting on going with her to protect her, so she was left with only one choice. "I'm beat," she told him. "I think I'll take a bath and turn in early. I didn't get enough sleep last night."

The second the words were out of her mouth, she wanted to sink right through the floor. He didn't say a word, but then again, he didn't have to. In the time it took for his eyes to meet hers, they were both thinking about last night and the bliss they'd found in each other's arms.

Heat climbing in her cheeks, she turned away, only

to frown when she saw the towels hanging on the towel rack outside the bathroom door. "Looks like you're going to have to air dry," she told him. "The maid only left one set of clean towels when she cleaned the room this morning."

Rolling his eyes, he growled, "It figures. Go ahead and use what we've got. I'll go get some more."

Grabbing the old-fashioned brass key, he headed for the office, giving Priscilla the time to herself she'd thought she so desperately needed. But as the silence closed around her and she sank into her solitary bath a few minutes later, Donovan was right there in her thoughts, whispering in her ear, reminding her that she wasn't going to be able to avoid him for long—the room only had one bed and they were sharing it.

Swearing softly at the thought, she told herself that tonight there wasn't going to be a replay of last night. She wasn't making love with him. Not yet. Possibly never again. She had to have a better handle on her emotions, had to know that when this was all over, life returned to normal, and they walked away from each other, he didn't take her heart with him.

She'd always considered herself pretty tough when it came to protecting herself. But when she finished her bath and stepped out of the bathroom, Donovan was stretched out on his stomach in the middle of the bed, sound asleep with his head cushioned on the towels he'd gotten at the motel office. Stopping in her tracks, she felt her heart turn over. How could the man look so incredibly sexy when he was asleep, for heaven's sake? It wasn't fair that he could steal her breath and make her weak at the knees at one and the same time, and he wasn't even aware of it!

Not sure if she was irritated or relieved, she almost woke him to tell him to quit hogging the bed, but it had been a long day for both of them, and he was obviously exhausted. And did she really want to wake him, anyway? If she crawled in beside him, he wouldn't even know she was there. What was the harm?

The matter settled, she slipped under the covers and stretched out on the sliver of space he'd left her on the side of the mattress. Almost immediately, the masculine scent of him surrounded her, teasing her senses and stirring memories of last night. Every instinct she had warned her this was a mistake. Making love with him could so easily become a wonderful, addictive habit that she might not be able to walk away from. But she was so tired, and keeping her eyes open was becoming more impossible by the second. She'd just lie here a moment and rest her eyes, she promised herself sleepily. Then she'd kick Donovan out of the bed and have it all to herself. Images flashed before her closed eyes at the thought, drawing a smile from her. She was still smiling when she fell asleep.

Donovan had always considered himself a man who never let down his guard, especially when he was on a job. He slept with one eye—and one ear—open at all times, and he took pride in the fact that no one had ever snuck up on him. So even when he was dead to the world, no one was more surprised than he when he felt a soft, feminine body snuggle close.

His eyes flew open, but he didn't move so much as

a muscle. Where the hell was he? And who was hugging him like a teddy bear?

Then it hit him. Priscilla. A smile tugged at his mouth. He'd gone to the office for towels, but she was still in the bathtub when he returned, so he'd lain down while he waited for her. He didn't even remember falling asleep, let alone her coming out of the bathroom and crawling into bed with him. He must have been completely out of it.

He wasn't, however, asleep now, he silently acknowledged as she burrowed closer. He was wide awake, and she was boneless against him, with her face buried against his chest. Totally unaware of how she'd unconsciously sought his body warmth, she slept like the dead. And with every soft breath she expelled against the sensitive skin of his neck and chest, she heated his blood.

If he'd had any sense, he'd put some space between them, then find a way to go back to sleep. But he was only human, and with her so close, he didn't have a snowball's chance in hell of pulling away. She just felt too good.

Later, he couldn't say when he knew she was awake. One minute, she was practically snoring, and the next, she stiffened ever so slightly. He could almost read her mind as she realized she was pressed up against him and she didn't have a clue how she'd gotten there.

Almost immediately, she started to withdraw, but his arms tightened around her before she could pull away. "Don't," he said huskily. "You're fine right where you are."

"We can't be lovers," she murmured.

"We already are."

"Just once. We don't have to compound the mistake."

"Who said it was a mistake?" he challenged. "I thought it was great."

When she hesitated, silence stretched between them like eternity. Not sure if he should be insulted or amused, Donovan didn't think she was going to respond at all when she suddenly said quietly, "It was."

"So what's the problem?"

"We're not friends."

She'd left the bathroom light on and the door slightly ajar, and in the dim light, she could see the wicked glint of amusement in his eyes even though he tried to adopt a hurt look at her words. "You don't like me?"

Biting back a smile, she said, "I didn't say that."

"You said we're not friends. Personally, I don't know how you can say that. I can make you laugh and protect you from the bad guys and take you all over the world. And when you need to be kissed, I kiss you," he added. "What more could you want?"

She lifted a brow at that. "*You kiss me when I need to be kissed?*"

"Absolutely," he said, and leaned close to softly brush her lips with his.

When he pulled back slightly and smiled into her eyes, he melted her heart. "Donovan—"

"Give me one good reason why we shouldn't do this."

What was she supposed to say to that? "Because…"

He kissed the side of her neck, and that was as far as she got. Her thoughts scrambled, and she couldn't stop herself from sighing in pleasure. "I can't think when you do that."

"I know," he said, and kissed her again. "If you come up with something, though, feel free to speak up."

She tried, but how was she supposed to think when he could disarm her with just a kiss? A touch? His hands trailed over her, tracing her curves, and suddenly, she was aching for the feel of his skin against hers. With a murmur, she reached for the buttons of his shirt, the snap of his jeans.

"You have too many clothes on," she complained. "Why did you go to bed with your jeans on? That can't be comfortable."

His hands one step ahead of hers, he dealt with the buttons on his shirt while she was still dealing with the snap on his jeans. "I just lay down to wait for you to get out of the bathroom," he reminded her as he set her hands from him and stepped from the bed, but only long enough to strip out of his clothes. "The next thing I knew, I was out like a light."

Slipping back into bed, he reached for her. "Now that we have that settled, I have a question."

How could he expect her to answer questions when he was naked in bed and touching her? she wondered, melting against him. When he traced the strap of her nightgown across her shoulder to the neckline and across the top of her breasts, she couldn't breathe, let alone concentrate.

When her only answer was a soft moan, he growled, "Are you particularly attached to this gown?"

Lost to everything but the feel of him under her hands and mouth, she kissed the side of his neck. "What gown?"

His chuckle turned into a groan as she kissed her

way up his neck and nibbled on his ear. "Witch," he rasped, and pulled her gown over her head and sent it flying across the room. A split second later, he grabbed her and rolled with her on the bed.

Her laughter mingled with his, but as he rolled to a stop with her on top, her breath caught in her throat as his fingers reached for her breasts. Need tightened deep in her belly, sweet and hot, and she shuddered.

He didn't have to ask what his touch did to her—he could feel it, see it in her eyes. And she had no idea what that did to him. There were no secrets to Priscilla Wyatt. Her emotions were right there in her eyes for the entire world to see, and she made no apologies for that. There were no games, no subterfuge, no lies. And for a man who dealt with liars, cowards and outlaws on the run, her honesty was not only a rare commodity but incredibly seductive. How was she still walking around free?

Her eyes searching his, she frowned. "What are you thinking?"

"Have you been living in a cave?"

"No, of course not." She laughed, surprised. "You know where I live—you've been there."

"Then the men in England must be idiots."

He could see the delight that surged into her eyes as she nodded in understanding. "I think so, too, but I didn't realize you were so discerning."

"Minx!" He laughed, and dragged her down to him for a quick kiss.

Chuckling, she kissed him back, but the heat that was burning deep in both of them refused to be contained any longer. His laughter faded, as did hers, and with a groan that seemed to come from his soul, he took the kiss deeper.

One kiss led to another, one touch to many, until time blurred and need clawed at them with silky sharp talons. Within minutes, they were both wound tighter than a broken watch.

Fighting the need to push them both over the edge, Donovan wanted to draw out the pleasure until they both forgot their own names, but Priscilla had other plans. She pushed him to his back and moved over him, stroking, teasing, driving him out of his mind with nothing more than her delicate, artistic fingers. Then, just when he was sure he couldn't stand the pleasure another instant, she trailed kisses right down the center of his chest. Just that easily, he lost it.

When Donovan's cell phone rang at three-forty in the morning, he woke with a start to find the covers on the floor, Priscilla draped across his chest, and her breathing soft and warm in his ear. He'd never been more content in his life. The last thing he wanted to do was get out of bed and retrieve his phone from where he'd left it on the chest to answer what was, no doubt, a wrong number. The Wyatts wouldn't call—they knew the phones were being tapped—so who else would be calling him, especially in the middle of the night?

Swearing, he gently rolled Priscilla off him, and wasn't surprised when she woke almost immediately. Rubbing her eyes, she frowned up at him in confusion. "Is it time to get up? Oh, my God! The phone! Who would be calling at this time of night?"

"It's probably a wrong number," he told her. "Some drunk who transposed the numbers."

But when he snatched up the phone and checked the caller ID, his expression turned grim. "It's Buck."

Priscilla turned white as a sheet. "Wh-what?! But he's not supposed to call us unless there's an emergency!"

When the phone rang again, Donovan wanted to reach for her, to comfort her, to assure her that there was no reason to panic, but he knew Buck wouldn't take a chance and call unless something was seriously wrong. Flipping open the phone, he braced for trouble. "What's wrong?"

"Someone just called and told me Priscilla was dead," Buck said tersely. "Dammit, Donovan, if she's hurt and you didn't call—"

"She's fine," he assured him. "She's right here next to me. Here—talk to her."

Concerned, Priscilla quickly took the phone. "Buck? It's me. I'm fine. Why would you think I'm not?"

"Because some jackass just called and said you were dead," he retorted, furious. "I know it was a trick, but I had to make sure. Dammit to hell! Now whoever's tapping the damn line is going to figure out where you are, and you're going to have to move again. I'm sorry, Sis. I couldn't go back to sleep without knowing that you're all right."

Tears welled in her eyes at his words. When was this nightmare going to be over? And when was the bastard who was torturing her family going to pay for all the horrible things he'd done?

"Don't you dare apologize. This isn't your fault. If we're going to blame someone, it's the monsters who are bullying us. And it's not going to work. Do you hear me, bastards?" she demanded furiously of their eavesdropper. "You want to listen? Listen to this! You're wasting your time, but go ahead and knock yourselves out. Throw all your dirty, nasty, underhanded tricks at us. They're not going to work. We're not leaving the ranch, and at the end of the month, it will officially be ours.

"Then we're going after you," she promised silkily. "And when we find out who you are, your ass is going to prison. We'll make sure of it."

"We'll show them as much mercy as they've shown us," Buck added grimly. "In the meantime, stay safe. Okay?"

"I will," she promised, blinking back tears. Why was she only now realizing how homesick she was for her family? "Tell Katherine and Elizabeth I miss you all, and I'll see you soon." Too choked up to say another word, she handed the phone to Donovan and turned away.

"I'm doing everything I can to keep her safe," he told Buck quietly. "And we haven't had any problems for a couple of days."

"Then I call and mess everything up," Buck said in disgust. "I'm sorry, man. Now you're going to have to move again."

"It's okay," Donovan assured him. "I don't like to stay in one place too long, anyway."

"I won't ask where you're going—I don't want to know. Just keep Cilla safe and show up here at the end of the month."

"I'll do that," Donovan said. "How are things at the ranch?" When Buck hesitated, he frowned. "That bad?"

"It's no more than we expected," he replied. "We're hanging tough. And staying at home," he added. "So far, we've all been here every night."

It was going to get worse before it got better, but Donovan knew he didn't have to tell Buck that. He, like Priscilla and her sisters, lived with the pressure of meeting the terms of Hilda's will every day. "If things get worse and you need us to come in, call," he said gruffly. "We'll be there as quickly as we can."

"If it looks like we're going to miss a night, I'll call you immediately," he promised. "Now go pack. You've got to move."

He didn't have to tell Donovan twice. Already plotting where they would go, he hung up and turned to find Priscilla hurriedly getting dressed. The tears he'd seen in her eyes earlier were gone, and in their place was outrage.

"You're mad," he told her as he pulled on jeans and a clean shirt. "Good. You need to be. That's what's going to get you through this."

"They're not going to beat us," she vowed, jerking a clean sweater over her head. "I don't care how much money or power they have or what kind of strings they can pull. Whoever is terrorizing us is wasting their time. They're not going to win this fight."

"Trust me—they're beginning to realize that," he replied. "That's why they're turning up the heat." Stepping into his boots, he tossed their suitcases onto the bed and began throwing clothes into them.

"We're tougher than they gave us credit for."

"But they have desperation on their side," he warned. "Don't make the mistake of thinking you've got this thing in the bag because you've been able to outsmart them so far. This war is far from over."

In the process of collecting shampoo, toothpaste and deodorant from the bathroom, she gave him a sharp look as she dumped it into the suitcases. "What are you saying? That they're going to get nastier? How can they? They've thrown everything but the kitchen sink at us already, and we've still managed to keep the ranch and evade them. What else can they do?"

"Don't ask," he retorted. "What's the ranch worth?"

She frowned. "I don't know. It's thousands of acres. What's that got to do with anything?"

"Humor me," he said. "So you own—or will at the end of the month—thousands of acres of prime Colorado ranch land. Sight unseen, I would guess it has to be worth a couple of million, at the very least. Wouldn't you say?"

She shrugged. "Maybe. Maybe more—I don't know. This isn't about the money."

"It's always about the money," he said dryly. "Trust me. If it was only worth a grand or two, no one would be fighting you and your family for the ranch. You're talking about millions, sweetheart. There are people who would sell their soul for something worth that kind of money."

She paled at that. "Do you really think they would go so far as to kill us?"

He didn't want to scare her, but she had to know what they were up against. "I don't know," he said grimly. "Someone has gone to a hell of a lot of trouble to drive the four of you away from the ranch, and they're running out of time. If they're desperate enough—and convinced that they really are the unnamed heir in Hilda's will—yes, I think they would find a way to justify homicide. Especially," he added, "since they've managed to repeatedly attack all of you and the ranch without getting caught. What have they got to be afraid of? No one has a clue who they are."

Shaken, Priscilla threw the last of their things in the suitcases and zipped them shut. "Let's get out of here."

It wasn't until they hurried out to the car, however, that Priscilla saw the lights on in the diner across the street and realized they were supposed to show up for work in less than fifteen minutes. "Oh, my God. Harry! We can't drive off without at least giving him some kind of explanation."

"The hell we can't," Donovan snapped as he threw the suitcases in the trunk. "He'll understand—"

"How can he when he won't have a clue why we didn't show up?" she argued. "We should at least tell him there's been an emergency or something and we have to leave. It won't take two seconds," she added quickly before he could disagree. "We can just slip in the back door, tell him goodbye, and leave."

After everything she'd been through, Donovan had to admit that she didn't ask for much. "All right." He sighed. "But you've got five seconds. That's it. Understood?"

He knew grown men who quaked in their shoes when he used that tone of voice. She only grinned and kissed him on the cheek.

"What do you mean…you're *quitting?*" Harry demanded. "Now?!"

"Something's come up," Priscilla said quickly. "We have to go—"

"You're running from something, aren't you? Someone's after you."

It wasn't a question but a flat statement of fact. Horrified that he had guessed, Priscilla stuttered, "N-no, of c-course not."

"I got a job offer in Seattle," Donovan lied. "It starts tomorrow, so we're going to have to haul ass if we're going to make it."

Priscilla had to give Donovan credit—he was totally believable. But Harry wasn't born yesterday and obviously knew a line of bull when he heard one. "If you don't want to tell me the truth, I understand," he said gruffly. "But you have nothing to fear from me. As far as I'm concerned, I never met anyone matching your descriptions, and I certainly don't know anyone with your names—"

"Or any other names," Donovan said pointedly.

Harry didn't even blink. "My cook, Justin, and my waitress, Mary Lou, had worked for me for two years and they just decided to run off and get married. Last I heard, they got jobs in Vegas and decided not to come back."

Donovan grinned. "Justin and Mary Lou, huh? We'll keep an eye out for them."

"You just keep Mary Lou safe," he said sternly.

Tears misting her eyes, Priscilla gave him a quick hug. "Under all that gruffness, you're a real softie."

Color singed his cheeks, and for just a second, his lips twitched and threatened to stretch into a smile. He scowled, but could do nothing about the twinkle in his eye. "Don't spread that around, okay?"

"We won't tell a soul," she promised.

Stepping over to the cash register, he quickly counted out their pay for the days they'd worked. "If you ever need a job, I'm here. Now get out of here before whoever's after you finds you."

He didn't have to tell them twice. Hurrying out to the car, they were the one of only three cars on the street at that hour of the morning, and the other cars were headed in the opposite direction. Keeping a watchful eye on the rearview mirror, Donovan turned right at the next corner and headed west.

"It looks like we're safe so far," Priscilla said quietly, glancing over her shoulder at the empty road behind them. "How long do you think we have before we have to worry about trouble showing up?"

He'd been wondering that himself. "If we're lucky, whoever's tapping the phones won't find out about Buck's call until much later this morning. By then, we'll be at least a hundred fifty miles or more from Los Angeles and no one will have a clue where to look for us."

He didn't tell Priscilla, but he would have felt a lot safer if there'd been more traffic at that hour of the morning. They weren't being followed—yet—but they stuck out like a sore thumb on the empty street. The faster they got away from the area, the better.

Normally he stuck to back roads when he was trying to evade someone, but not this time. Interstate 5 was less than a mile away and offered a quick escape. They'd head north toward Hollywood and then just pick an exit and disappear. Maybe they'd go further north and go all the way up to Carmel. It was a beautiful drive along the coast, and he'd show Priscilla—

A half mile down the road, the flashing lights of several patrol cars caught his attention. They appeared to stretch across the road and block traffic on all sides. "What the hell!"

Following his gaze, Priscilla gasped. "Oh, my God! Is it an accident? But no one's on the road!"

Never taking his eyes from the flashing lights in the predawn darkness, Donovan swore. "That's not an accident. It's a roadblock."

"A roadblock? What? You mean like a license check?"

"No, it's a hell of a lot more serious than that. My guess is they're looking for someone."

Stunned, Priscilla frowned. "Who?"

"Us."

Chapter 11

"Hang on, sweetheart. We're going for a ride," he warned, and took a sharp right at the next corner. Not surprised when he heard sirens almost immediately, Donovan raced around another corner before their pursuers even turned down the first side street they'd taken.

Beside him, Priscilla was as white as a sheet as the sound of the sirens grew closer. "Why are they after us? We haven't done anything."

"That's a damn good question," he said grimly. Flattening the accelerator all the way to the floor, he raced through the darkened residential streets as fast as he dared. "How the hell could whoever's after the ranch persuade the Los Angeles police to set up a roadblock for us?"

"Someone couldn't just call and lie and say we were bank robbers or something?"

"Whoever arranged this definitely lied, but it's not that simple," he replied. "Only a law enforcement agency can issue an APB—and they're not going to do that just because someone comes crying to them with a bunch of lies. They'd have to have a reason—"

"Unless someone in law enforcement or a position of authority is the one lying," she pointed out.

The truth hit them both like a slap in the face. "It's someone in the police department—"

"Or a judge," he cut in, cursing. "Dammit, I should have seen it the second I realized the phones were tapped. It takes a court order to tap a phone. And if a judge went to the police and requested an APB, especially in a small town like Willow Bend where everyone knows everyone else, the police probably aren't going to ask too many questions."

"Especially if they're all part of the conspiracy to drive us away from the ranch," she added, horrified. "We've got to call Buck. He has to know what's going on, that he can't trust anyone, not even the cops or the judges."

"Not yet," Donovan said. "The call will be traced the second you make it, so let's get to the other side of town first and make a few preparations."

"What kind of preparations?"

"You'll see," he promised, and once again made a series of quick turns that took them farther from the roadblock and their pursuers. Forced to go the speed limit, he wound through residential streets, onto main thoroughfares and back to residential streets, heading north, then east, always keeping his eyes peeled for the police as he waited for the morning rush hour to start.

He didn't have long to wait. By the time he zipped onto the Santa Ana Freeway, dawn was still an hour away, but thousands of drivers were already on the road. Blending in with the other vehicles, Donovan didn't even blink when they passed a patrol car. Earlier, when he'd evaded the roadblock, the police hadn't been able to see what kind of car he and Priscilla were in. And they obviously still didn't know. The policeman they passed didn't even look twice at them.

When he took a random exit on the north side of Los Angeles and pulled into a Wal-Mart parking lot, Priscilla looked at him in surprise. "Why are we stopping here? I thought we were going to get out of town."

"We are. But first we're going to buy a tape recorder. Then we're going to call Buck."

"Without it being traced?"

"No, but that's okay," he assured her. "This is one call we want to be traced."

Forty minutes later, Donovan called Buck's number, then quickly laid his cell phone on the tape recorder he'd placed under some landscape bushes in the parking lot of one of Los Angeles's largest shopping malls. Just as he heard Buck answer, he hit the Play button on the tape recorder, then hurried over to where Priscilla waited in the running car fifty feet away.

"I know we'd agreed to no contact," his recorded message said, "but just listen. Okay? Something happened this morning you need to know about. Less than an hour after we spoke this morning, we were nearly caught in a police roadblock. We're fine and still on the run, but you and the girls need to realize that the authorities are involved in this. I'm talking judges, police, anyone with any authority in Willow Bend. Do not trust anyone! Whoever called in an APB on us is either in the police department or working with someone who is. And a judge had to order the wiretap. He could have been acting on false information given to him or done this on his own. Either way, the three of you can't trust anyone but each other. Understood? Please be careful. We won't be calling anymore. It's just too dangerous. If there's anything we need to know, send me an e-mail. I'll try to check it somewhere along the way. Priscilla's fine. She's just worried about you."

That was a huge understatement. Priscilla was, in fact, nearly sick with worry as Donovan sent the car racing onto the entrance ramp of the freeway that bordered one side of the mall, leaving his cell phone and the tape recorder far behind. "Are you sure he got the message?" she asked worriedly. "What if he hung up before the message started to play?"

"I heard him answer," Donovan told her. "And even if there was a slight delay between the time he answered and the start of the message, he knew the call was from me. He wouldn't have hung up."

Suddenly chilled, she asked. "How long do you think it will take the police to show up at the mall?"

He shrugged. "An hour? Maybe less. It doesn't really matter. They don't know what we're driving or where we're headed."

"Where *are* we headed?"

"Colorado."

"What?! Why?"

Donovan hadn't intended to tell her, at least not yet, but she had a right to know just what kind of danger her family was in. "Whoever's tapping Buck's phone heard the message we left, sweetheart. They know that Buck is aware of the fact that whoever is orchestrating all this is a hell of a lot more well connected than any of you dreamed."

She paled. "And you think they'll come after him before he can tell anyone?"

"It's a possibility," he said grimly. "They're not going to take a chance on him or anyone else in the family going to the FBI. They'll throw everything they've got at the ranch, which is why we're heading for Colorado. If your family needs us, we'll be close by."

Alarmed, Priscilla said, "Can't you go faster?"

"Not without speeding." Reaching across the console, he took her hand and linked her fingers with his. "We'll get there as fast as we can, sweetheart, but we can't take a chance on getting stopped by a state trooper. There's no telling what kind of story has been put out there about us. The last thing we want is to get arrested."

She hadn't even thought of that. "But we haven't done anything! And we're using aliases."

"Trust me—pictures went out with those APBs. And," he added bluntly, "a dirty cop doesn't need us to do anything wrong to make it look like we did. Whatever charges he sent out with the APBs were nothing but lies. These bastards write their own rules, sweetheart, so don't expect anyone to play fair. It's not going to happen."

She knew he was only giving her the worst case scenario just in case things went south. It didn't, unfortunately, help. More afraid than ever for her family, she did the only thing she could. She prayed.

They drove all day and into the night. Priscilla offered to drive when they stopped to get some coffee, but Donovan wasn't willing to risk it. "You haven't had enough driving experience in the U.S.," he retorted. "This isn't the time to get it."

"But you've got to be exhausted," she protested.

"I'm fine," he assured her. "The coffee helps."

"Yeah, right," she sniffed. "That's why your eyes are burning."

Surprised, he looked at her in the darkness. "How did you know my eyes were burning?" When she just looked at him, he sighed. "Okay, you're right. Satisfied? I'm still not letting you drive."

"Be that way," she said with a shrug. "I guess I'll just have to keep you awake with stories about my childhood."

"Oh, God," he groaned. "Anything but that!"

"I'll have you know I was a cute kid," she retorted, fighting a smile.

"I'll bet you were a sissy. You took dance lessons, didn't you? You probably had a pink ballerina outfit and danced around on your toes all the time?"

"Me?" She laughed. "Not hardly. I was a tomboy."

"Yeah, right," he snorted. "That's a whopper if I ever heard it."

"No, really. I learned to ride a bike when I was four—"

"That doesn't make you a tomboy. Anybody can ride a bike."

"Okay, smarty pants, I'll agree with you on that. But sissies don't jump out of a tree house when they're five and break their ankle."

Surprised, he shot her a sharp look. "You had a tree house?"

She nodded, smiling at the memory. "My mother designed it, and my grandfather built it. It was like something out of an old Tarzan movie. It had bedrooms, ceiling fans—even running water."

"You're making that up."

"I am not. Honest. It was incredible."

As the miles passed and they reached the Colorado state line, she told him about the summer art classes where she first fell in love with designing, the trips to Paris with her mother, where they went shopping and to fashion shows, and she left her tomboy ways behind, the dreams her mother encouraged her to follow.

Closing her eyes, remembering, she smiled sleepily. "I really had a wonderful childhood. I just wish my mother had lived to see how far I've come with my designs. She would have been thrilled."

"When did she die?"

"Five years ago," she said quietly. "She and my dad were killed in a car accident one night when they were coming home from a party. It was the worst night of all of our lives."

Suddenly realizing that while she had been reminiscing with her eyes closed, the tiredness she had been fighting for hours caught up with her. Try as she may, she couldn't seem to stay awake. "I'm sorry," she said huskily, sitting straighter in her seat. "I'm supposed to help keep you awake and I can't keep my eyes open."

"You're doing fine," he told her with a chuckle. "Anyway, we'll be there soon. That's the lights of Colorado Springs on the horizon."

That brought her eyes open as nothing else could. "Colorado Springs! Why are we going there? I thought we were going to Willow Bend."

"Not yet," he said. "It's too dangerous. First we have to get some backup."

She frowned. "What do you mean?"

"The FBI. One of my friends—Carlos Rodriquez—is the head of the local office."

"But Colorado Springs isn't really that far from Willow Bend. What if your friend is somehow in on all this? We'll be jumping from the frying pan into the fire."

"Carlos is straight as an arrow," he assured her. "If anyone can find out what's going on in Willow Bend, he can."

Priscilla wanted to believe him, but she couldn't forget how whoever was after the ranch had connections that reached all the way to London. What if Donovan was wrong? What then? When was this nightmare going to end?

"It's the middle of the night," she said as anxiety sent goose bumps racing over her skin. "How do you even know he's here? He could be on assignment. Or he might not even work for the FBI anymore. When was the last time you talked to him?"

"Two weeks ago. And no, he's not in the office at this time of night, but I have his home phone number.

I'll call him as soon as we get in town and see if he can meet us somewhere." At her silence, he squeezed her hand. "It's going to be all right, Priscilla. I would never do anything to hurt you or your family."

"I know that," she said softly. "It's just so hard to have any faith in law enforcement anymore. You don't know who the good guys are." Suddenly remembering the betrayal in his own past, she frowned at him searchingly. "Dirty cops nearly destroyed your life. How did you ever get past that?"

"I'm still suspicious as hell of anyone with a badge," he admitted. "Obviously, there are people like Carlos who I trust, but that didn't happen overnight. He had to prove himself to me."

If he trusted this Carlos person that much, she had to trust his judgment. That didn't mean, however, that she wasn't anxious when Donovan stopped at a truck stop on the outskirts of Colorado Springs to call him.

"He's going to open the office up for us," he said as he rejoined her a few minutes later. "There'll be no one there but the three of us. If there's a dirty cop in the office, he won't even know we've been there. Okay?"

Relieved, she sighed. "Okay."

Fifteen minutes later, they arrived at the federal building to find Carlos Rodriquez waiting for them at the entrance. Extending his hand to Priscilla as Donovan introduced them, he grinned. "You must be a saint if you can hang around with this wild man for any length of time without killing him."

"I've considered it a few times," she admitted with a smile. "It's nice to meet you."

"Hopefully, I can help you. C'mon up to the office, and you can tell me what's going on."

Once inside, they took the elevator up to the third floor, and within minutes, he'd made coffee, collected a notepad and a tape recorder and showed them into a small conference room. "Okay," he said as he took a seat across the table from them. "What's going on?"

"Eleven months ago, my brother and sisters and I inherited the Broken Arrow Ranch near Willow Bend," Priscilla told him. "Our cousin, Hilda Wyatt, left it to us, but she must have been afraid that we wouldn't actually live there since we're from England, so one of the requirements of the inheritance is that one of us has to be at the ranch every night for a year. We can be absent for one night without any penalty, but not two consecutive nights."

Taking notes, Carlos looked up curiously. "What's the penalty?"

"The ranch goes to an unnamed heir."

"And who knows about this clause?"

"Apparently, at least half of Colorado."

He whistled softly. "Let me guess—half of Colorado has been trying to drive you away."

"Oh, it gets better than that," she said and proceeded to tell him about the attacks on the ranch and the family.

"And whoever's doing this isn't limiting the attacks to the Willow Bend area," Donovan added darkly. "Someone deliberately ran into Priscilla's car in London, and then when she got out of the hospital, they kidnapped her. That's when I came on the scene. Her brother hired me to track her down and keep her safe until the year is up at the end of the month and the ranch is theirs."

Taking notes furiously, Carlos frowned. "What the hell have the police been doing while all this was going on? There must have been evidence... suspects...*something!*"

"Most of the time, there wasn't any evidence at all," Priscilla said in disgust. "And when there were any leads, nothing came of them."

"That's not the worst of it," Donovan told him. "Someone put a wiretap on her brother's phone."

Stunned, Carlos snapped, "Who the hell ordered that? And why? What grounds did the police have for a wiretap?"

"That's why we're here," he replied. "We were hoping you could tell us."

Sitting back in his chair, he studied Donovan with sharp, brown eyes. "How do you know for sure there's a wiretap?"

"Because someone has chased us all the way from London, and every time we lost them, they'd find us again when we talked to Buck."

"Then they're not just tapping the phones, they've got to be using global positioning on your cell to find you."

"I don't see any other explanation," Donovan agreed. "They almost caught us in Los Angeles this morning less than an hour after Buck called. An hour, dammit. In Los Angeles! That's not dumb luck. Especially when the police set up a roadblock."

That got Carlos's attention, just as Donovan knew it would. "What the hell! How do you know they were after you?"

"Because it was four o'clock in the morning," he retorted. "When was the last time you heard of a road-block being set up at four in the morning?"

"It happens," he argued. "There could have been a robbery, a murder, a cop down and the perp still in the area."

"Was there?" Priscilla asked.

"There's only one way to find out," he said, and moved to the computer on the desk in the corner.

Sitting back in his chair at the table, Donovan watched as Carlos checked the LAPD records, as well as all APBs issued in Colorado and California and the adjoining states. When he swore, Donovan knew he'd hit pay dirt. "Well?"

"The phone tap was ordered by a Judge Garrison in Willow Bend," he told them. "And it looks like the APB came from there, also. Don't jack with me, Donovan. Is there any reason the police would be after you or Priscilla?"

"No, of course not. You know me, Carlos. I don't do that kind of crap."

"You're sure? You don't have any outstanding warrants? Maybe something you forgot about?"

"I haven't even gotten a traffic ticket in eight years," Donovan insisted. "Trust me. There's nothing."

"We did use fake passports to get into the country," Priscilla admitted. "But there's no way a judge from Willow Bend would know that."

Not sure if he wanted to laugh or groan, Donovan said, "Sweetheart, you don't tell an FBI agent you got into the country illegally."

"It wasn't illegally," she said defensively. "I had my

real passport, and you did, too. We just didn't use them. We couldn't," she told Carlos. "My kidnappers tracked us all over England. We couldn't take a chance that they would follow us to the United States, so we used false names...and fake passports. What else were we supposed to do? We didn't know who we could trust."

Struggling to hold back a smile, Carlos said, "We'll deal with that later. For now, you're right. A judge in Willow Bend wouldn't have a clue how you got into the country. What I want to know is why he authorized a phone tap and who requested it. Something doesn't smell right."

"So you're going to check it out?" Donovan asked.

He nodded. "In the meantime, I want you to stay as far away from Willow Bend and Judge Garrison as possible and let me handle this."

"We can't," Priscilla said, stricken. "The ranch is scheduled to officially become ours at the end of the month. Between now and then, whoever is after the Broken Arrow is going to throw everything they can at my family, and they've got no one they can call on for help, no one they can trust. I'm not going to hide in the shadows while they go through hell. I have to go home."

"If you really want to help your family," Carlos said, "give me some time to investigate and find out who's behind this. That's the only way to put a stop to it."

"I can't," she said simply, rising to her feet. "My family needs me."

Donovan had to agree with her. "Thanks, man," he told Carlos as he, too, came to his feet. "I'll be in touch. With the wiretap, you can't call us at the ranch, and I left my old cell phone in California to throw off whoever's tracking us. As soon as I get a new one, I'll call you and give you the number."

Not happy with their decision, he commanded, "Just be careful, okay? I'm going to get on this immediately, but it's still going to take some time to get some answers. Don't do anything stupid."

"I'm going to make sure we're ready for just about anything the bastards can throw at us," Donovan said coldly, "but we're not going to sneak into town like we've got something to hide. The more people who know we're coming, the safer we'll be."

"I agree," Carlos said, "but I still don't like it. If you run into something you can't handle, call me."

Donovan liked to think there wasn't much on this earth that he couldn't handle if he had time to prepare for it, but life didn't always turn out the way you expected. Two hours later, they were ten miles from Willow Bend when they stopped at a truck stop to call Buck.

"What's wrong?" Buck demanded the second Donovan said hello and he recognized his voice. "Is Priscilla all right?"

"She's fine. She's coming home."

"What?! No!"

"She's not going to leave you to fight this fight alone," Donovan said gruffly. "We'll be there in fifteen minutes or so." Suddenly hearing a siren, he turned in time to see a sheriff's patrol car race into the truck stop parking lot with lights flashing. And it was heading straight for where he stood with Priscilla at the pay phone. "What the hell!" he growled. "I've got to go, Buck."

"Wait! You—"

"I'll call you back," he promised. Hanging up, he stepped protectively in front of Priscilla and faced the older man who stepped out of the car. "Can I help you, sheriff?"

"I need to see your driver's license," he said coolly. "And yours, too, Miss Wyatt."

Behind him, Donovan felt Priscilla crowd closer to him before she gathered the courage to face the sheriff. Stepping around him, she confronted the older man. "I beg your pardon? My name is—"

"Priscilla Wyatt," he answered for her. "And this," he continued, looking pointedly at Donovan, "is the man you've been on the run with."

"On the run?" Donovan said and laughed. "What are you talking about? The last I checked, she was over twenty one and free to go wherever she wanted."

"Not when she deliberately avoids a license check," he retorted. "You're both under arrest."

"What the hell!"

"You can't be serious! It wasn't even a license check. It was an ambush—"

Too late, she realized she'd given away too much information, and she wanted to kick herself. The sheriff couldn't have known for sure that they'd been in Los Angeles. The authorities never even got a look at the vehicle they were driving, let alone saw their faces.

"What do you mean it was an ambush?" he demanded. "Who was ambushing you?"

"I don't know," she replied, fighting the urge to run. "Forget I said anything—"

"The hell I will," he retorted. "You don't make a claim like that without reason. Who's ambushing you?"

Trapped, she was left with no choice but to answer him. "Judge Garrison. He ordered wiretaps on our phones."

Looking at her as if she were crazy, he snapped, "That's the craziest thing I ever heard of. Judge Garrison has an impeccable reputation. Who told you that nonsense?"

In for a penny, in for a pound, she thought, and told him the truth. "The FBI."

Chapter 12

"You're still under arrest," Sheriff Clark told them coldly. "If you're telling the truth, I'll release you after I talk to the FBI, but in the meantime, I'm not taking any chances."

Priscilla couldn't believe he was serious. "It was a license check, for heaven's sake! You don't arrest people for that."

"I can arrest you for any damn thing I like," he sneered. And before she could guess his intentions, he pulled out a pair of handcuffs and slapped them on her left wrist. "You're under arrest," he repeated. "What you say can and will be used against you in a court of law. If you cannot afford an attorney, one will be appointed for you—"

"We get the gist of it," Donovan cut in as he started to pull Priscilla's hands behind her back. "Do you really think it's necessary to cuff her behind her back, Sheriff? It's not like she's an ax murderer or anything. She's unarmed, for God's sake."

His face set in hard lines, the older man hesitated, then grudgingly gave in. "All right," he said as he secured Priscilla's hands in front of her and then did the same to Donovan. "But don't even think about trying anything just because I'm cutting you some slack. As far as I'm concerned, anyone who tries to avoid arrest is asking to be shot."

He didn't say he would shoot them, but Donovan didn't miss the not so subtle threat. And as he watched the old man through narrowed eyes, every instinct he had told him Sherm Clark was a little too close to the edge. One wrong move and they would find themselves looking down the barrel of his gun. Whether he would actually pull the trigger or not was still up for grabs, but Donovan wasn't willing to find out. He was a daredevil when it came to a hell of a lot of things, but he wasn't stupid enough to take his chances with a loaded gun or risk Priscilla getting shot.

"I agree," Donovan said. "So you don't have to worry about us. We're not going to try anything."

Beside him, Priscilla stood as still as stone, looking like a deer caught in the headlights. He wanted to tell her not to despair—he wasn't going to let anything happen to her—but he couldn't very well do that in front of the maniac sheriff. Instead, all he could say was, "We're not going to try anything. Right, sweetheart?"

She blinked, and the fear that had been in her eyes only seconds before was replaced with a healthy dose of outrage when she looked up at him and lied through her teeth. "No," she said stiffly. "Of course we're not going to try anything. We're not that stupid."

If he hadn't been cuffed, Donovan would have hugged her. Did she have any idea how proud of her he was? A lot of women would have fallen apart under such circumstances, but even though she was afraid, she was furious, and he thanked God for it. He needed her anger—her spunk to help him get them through this.

Jerking open the rear door of his patrol car, the sheriff motioned for them to get in the car. "Let's go."

With their hands cuffed in front of them, they slid into the backseat and heard the sheriff hit the door locks as he climbed behind the wheel. When he pulled out of the parking lot, Donovan expected him to turn east, toward Willow Bend. He turned west, instead.

Beside him, Priscilla stiffened. "This isn't the way to Willow Bend," she told the sheriff through the metal grillwork that held them captive in the backseat. "Where are you taking us?"

"I've got a stop to make before I head back to the office," he said, meeting her gaze in the mirror. "Not that I answer to you, Missy. If you know what's good for you, you'll sit there and keep your mouth shut."

She wanted to blast him—Donovan could feel the fury building in her, but she held her tongue. If looks could kill, though, the sheriff would have keeled over right then and there. And Donovan understood exactly how she felt. Before the day was through, the bastard would pay for speaking to her that way, he promised himself. He'd make sure of it. First, however, he had to free them from the handcuffs that held them captive.

Not for the first time over the course of the last fifteen

minutes, he marveled at the sheriff's cockiness…and stupidity. The jackass had been so anxious to slap cuffs on them and arrest them that he hadn't taken time to search them. And that was going to cost him.

Keeping his gaze lowered so that the sheriff couldn't see the satisfaction gleaming in his eyes, he slowly dropped his cuffed hands between his knees and carefully searched the hidden pocket in the top of his boot for the tools of the trade he never went anywhere without. Within seconds, he found what he was looking for. To the untrained eye, it looked like nothing more than a small piece of wire, but it could open almost anything. The trick was to do it without making a sound and alerting the sheriff to what he was doing.

Beside him, Priscilla shifted slightly in her seat, and his eyes met hers. She didn't say a word, but her gaze dropped to his hands. She knew exactly what he was up to, and she waited patiently for him to make his move.

Positioning the wire in the lock, he glanced up at the rearview mirror and said, "Do you usually take detainees with you when you've got another call, sheriff? We have a right to a lawyer—"

His gaze meeting his in the mirror, the sheriff laughed, completely unconcerned. "This is my county, son, and in case you haven't noticed, I'm in charge. The only way you're calling a lawyer is if I say you can call one, and that's not going to happen."

"So what…you're just going to lock us up and throw away the key?" he asked as the handcuffs soundlessly clicked open. "Do you really think you're going to get away with that? Priscilla's family is expecting us. They know she's in the area. There's no way in hell they're going to let her disappear off the face of the earth and not come looking for her."

Far from concerned, he only laughed again and seemed to have no idea that he sounded more than a little mad. "Do you really think I'm worried about the Wyatts? Nobody wants them here. Nobody will care when the rest of them end up dead, too."

"So you're going to kill us?" Donovan asked as he very carefully reached over and unlocked Priscilla's cuffs. "That's your plan? To take us out in the middle of nowhere and shoot us? Then when Priscilla's family shows up, you'll pick them off, one by one, won't you?"

The sheriff just shrugged. "Sounds like you've got it all figured out."

"Maybe," Donovan said. "So what are you going to tell the FBI? They'll show up, you know. We've already talked to them, and trust me, they're checking your ass out. And when we end up dead," he added, "they're going to shut down Willow Bend and take a good hard look at everyone. That includes you. Then what are you going to do? Claim that we tried to escape and you had no choice but to shoot us? What about the rest of the family? What excuse are you going to come up with for killing them?"

Sheriff Clark shrugged, unconcerned. "They snapped when they heard their darling baby sister was dead and came after me. I had to protect myself."

"Why are you doing this?" Priscilla cried. "This is crazy! What did we ever do to you? We don't even really know you."

"You took what was mine," he said coldly. "And for that, you're all going to pay."

"*Yours?* What are you talking about? We don't have anything that belongs to you."

"The hell you don't," he snarled. "The Broken Arrow is mine. Mine! And if you think I'm going to stand by and let you steal it right out from under me, then you obviously don't know who you're messing with. Nobody steals from me and gets away with it."

Priscilla and Donovan exchanged a glance and read each other's minds. He was crazy. There was no other explanation. Not to mention dangerous. If they were going to get out of this alive, they were going to have to be very, very careful.

For the moment, though, they were trapped in the back of the sheriff's patrol car. And even though their hands were now free, the doors were locked and controlled by the sheriff. Effectively caged, there was nothing they could do until he stopped and let them out. Donovan didn't even want to think about what their odds of survival were if he decided to shoot them right there in the car.

"If you don't mind me asking, sir, why do you think that the ranch should be yours?" Donovan asked. "From what I've heard, everyone in Willow Bend seems to think they're entitled to it."

"They're all fools," the older man retorted. "Tom Stevens, Rachel Carter, Michael Iverson, even Judge Garrison. They all thought they were so clever, but I knew everything they were doing—"

"And did nothing to stop it," Priscilla said bitterly. "What kind of sheriff are you?"

"Why would I stop them? They were damn helpful, even when they were amateurs and pretty much stuck to cutting fences and stealing cattle. Though Judge Garrison came in real handy when he ordered the wiretap," he added. "After that, I could keep track of everything going on at the ranch."

"So you and the judge were working together?" Donovan said. "What about the rest of the local law enforcement? Were the police helping you, too?"

"No one was knowingly helping me," he replied smugly. "They were all looking out for themselves...or so they thought. The poor fools never realized they were wasting their time. Just because Hilda Wyatt was friends with everyone in the county didn't mean she ever had any intention of leaving the Broken Arrow to anyone but family."

Donovan frowned. "If that's the case, then aren't you wasting your time, too? After all, you're not any more family than anyone else in Willow Bend. So why would Hilda make you the unnamed heir? Were you a special friend of hers or what?"

"No, we weren't friends," he snapped, fury flashing in his eyes. "We were a hell of a lot more than that. She was my mother!"

"She was not!" Priscilla said indignantly, shocked. "She never had any children. She was an old maid."

"She was raped when she was sixteen and got pregnant. She was sent to live with an aunt in California where she had me and then gave me up for adoption."

Stunned, Priscilla wanted to believe he was lying, that the wonderful woman who left the ranch to her and her siblings hadn't suffered the nightmare of a rape and then a pregnancy when she was barely more than a girl. But why would he make up such a thing?

He obviously was one step away from insanity, but his words had the ring of truth. And all she could think of was poor Hilda, who never married, never had another child, and had, obviously, never spoken of the rape to anyone outside her immediate family. If she had, the locals would have been only too eager to spread the word that Hilda had an illegitimate child who should inherit the ranch.

Blinking back tears, Priscilla could only imagine what a rape and unwanted pregnancy must have done to a young girl growing up in a small community in the 1930s. No wonder she never married. She must have hidden her secret all of her life and feared the day her child of rape showed up on her doorstep.

"You confronted her, didn't you?" she demanded. "You found out who she was, tracked her down and confronted her."

"You're damn straight I did," he growled. "She was my mother. I had a right to know her."

"And how did she react when you told her who you were?" Donovan asked.

"I'd been looking for her for years," he said bitterly, "and she acted like I was the one who raped her. She made me promise I would leave her alone and wouldn't tell anyone who I was."

"And you agreed?" Priscilla asked, surprised. "Just like that?"

"I did after she promised to leave the ranch to me," he retorted. "Lying bitch! She tricked me into staying away from her and then denied me my birthright. What kind of mother would do such a thing?"

The kind who obviously wanted no reminders of a

horrible rape, Priscilla thought, but that was something she kept to herself.

Snarling a curse, the sheriff hardly seemed aware of what he was confessing when he said half to himself, "I couldn't let her get away with that. I was a Wyatt. I deserved my share of the Broken Arrow, and she wasn't going to stop me from getting it. Nobody's going to stop me."

And with no other warning than that, he turned off the country road onto a dirt road that led into a canyon. And the deeper he raced into the canyon, the more the dirt road deteriorated. The undergrowth pushed in on them, and seconds later, they came to a dead end.

When the sheriff pushed open his door and stepped out of the patrol car, Priscilla paled. When he started to open her door, fear coiled through her. What now? she thought wildly. Was he going to dump them there and leave them in the middle of nowhere? Shoot them? Kill them?

"Don't let him see the cuffs are open," Donovan said in a hushed whisper. "Follow my lead."

She wanted to ask him how she was supposed to do that when she was scared out of her mind, but there was no time. Her door was jerked open and the sheriff bellowed, "Get out."

Shaking like a leaf, she did as he said, but it wasn't easy. She was wearing a long-sleeved sweater, and that helped hide the unlocked handcuffs draped loosely around her wrists, but with every move, she was terrified that they would clink together. Afraid he would notice, she said loudly, "Why have you brought us here? What do you want from us? We didn't write Hilda's will. If you want to blame someone, blame her."

"Oh, she's got her own special place in hell," he said coldly as Donovan stepped out of the car and joined her. "And so will the two of you and the rest of the Wyatts."

When he jerked his service revolver out of the holster on his hip, Donovan swore. "Are you sure you want to do this? Killing us won't accomplish anything, you know. There are three more Wyatts at the ranch. You can't kill all of them."

Madness gleaming in his eyes, Sherm Clark grinned maliciously. "Why can't I? And I can start with Miss Prissy here." In the blink of an eye, he pointed the gun straight at Priscilla. "Where would you like the first bullet, sweetheart? Your head or your heart? Or I can do both, one after the other. You won't feel a thing."

"Leave her alone, you bastard," Donovan growled.

The sheriff never took his eyes off Priscilla. "Go to hell."

Donovan told himself Clark was bitter and twisted, but he wasn't the kind who did his own dirty work. He stood back and let other people do that. He'd never have the nerve to kill someone himself.

But even as Donovan tried to convince himself the sheriff was just trying to scare them, the older man's face hardened. Something flickered in his cold blue eyes, something that turned Donovan's blood to ice. "No!"

Throwing his handcuffs at the older man, he jumped in front of Priscilla just as Sherm Clark dodged the handcuffs and pulled the trigger. Donovan felt the bullet, hotter than hell, slam into his shoulder, and sent up a silent prayer of thanks for the handcuffs. If he hadn't distracted him so he had to dodge the cuffs, he would have blown his head off.

"No!" Priscilla screamed when he was knocked off his feet. Throwing her own cuffs at the sheriff's head, she missed, but she hardly noticed. She couldn't take her eyes off Donovan.

"Get back!" the sheriff snarled when she took a step toward Donovan. "I mean it! You take three steps back or I'll blow your damn head off. Move. Now!" he cried, and aimed the revolver right at her head.

Pale as a ghost, she stepped back because he didn't give her any other choice. "Don't do this," she pleaded. "It isn't going to solve anything."

"Shut up!"

Hate etching his face, he took a step toward her, the gun never wavering as he pointed it at her head. Unable to take her gaze off the gun, Priscilla paled as his finger moved on the trigger. "No!"

Her scream echoed down the canyon just as two shots rang out. Petrified she waited for a bullet right between the eyes, but it was the sheriff who cried out when a slug slammed into his hand and his pistol went flying. A split second later, a second bullet caught him in the leg, and he screamed in pain.

Stunned, Priscilla didn't wait to see who had come to her rescue...or if whoever had shot the sheriff also intended to shoot her. It didn't matter. Nothing mattered but Donovan.

Rushing to his side, she dropped to her knees and was alarmed to see the blood streaming from the wound in his shoulder. "Oh, my God!"

"We've got to get out of here," he said tightly, struggling to sit up and wincing in pain. "We don't know where those shots came from."

"I don't give a damn where they came from," she retorted. "We've got to stop the bleeding before you bleed to death!"

"Let him bleed," the sheriff grumbled, trying to wrap a handkerchief around the wound in his calf. "He deserves it and so do you."

"Get the first aid kit out of the patrol car, sweetheart," Donovan told Priscilla. "And bring me the sheriff's gun. I don't trust the bastard."

She looked around for the gun and spied it on the ground, five feet from where Sherm Clark had fallen. Just as she hurried over to it, he lunged, scrambling for the gun.

It happened so fast, she didn't have time to think. "No!" she cried, and dove for the gun.

Caught up in the fight for control, she didn't hear Donovan curse or see him struggle to come to her aid. There was only the sheriff…and the gun. The thunder of her heart loud in her ears, she reached for the revolver, felt the cold metal under her fingers.

"Bitch!" Clark screamed and wrapped his fingers in her hair. Giving a fierce yank, he laughed as she gasped in pain.

Tears flooding her eyes, Priscilla wasn't going to let him win. Her scalp burning and her head jerked back at an excruciating angle, she threw the gun with all her might into the bushes ten feet away.

Bellowing in rage, the sheriff released her hair, only to backhand her across the face. Stars exploded in front of her eyes, then went black. Without a sound, she slid boneless to the ground.

"Priscilla? C'mon, sweetheart, open your eyes. You're going to be all right."

"It's over, Sis. Wake up. You're safe. We're all safe now."

From what seemed like a thousand miles away, Priscilla heard Donovan and her brother calling to her. She struggled through the blackness that engulfed her, only to moan as pain pulled at her, dragging her back to consciousness.

"My face hurts," she whispered. Barely able to open her eyes, she frowned in confusion at the sight of her brother and her soon to be brother-in-law, Hunter, flanking Donovan and hovering over her worriedly. "What happened? Where did you two come from?"

"After Donovan called and said you were on your way to the ranch, Buck was afraid you weren't going to make it safely, so we came looking for you," Hunter explained.

"We saw the sheriff stop you," Buck added, "and stayed back far enough that he wouldn't notice us trailing him. I think he was so excited about catching you that he completely forgot to check his mirrors. When he stopped and let the two of you out of the car, we were too far away to do anything when he shot Donovan."

At her brother's words, Priscilla gasped as the horror of the last hour came rushing back, and her eyes flew to Donovan's bloody shoulder. "Are you all right?" she asked him. "We've got to call an ambulance!"

"Two are on the way right now," Buck assured her. "One for you and Donovan and the other for the sheriff."

Outraged, she couldn't believe she'd heard him correctly. "You called an ambulance for that jackass? He shot Donovan! And hit me!"

"And Donovan beat the stuffing out of him," Hunter told her with a grin. "For a man with a bullet hole in his shoulder, he packs a whale of a punch. It took both of us to pull him off the jerk."

Surprised, she looked at Donovan with a new level of respect. "You hit him for me?"

His lips twitched slightly. "Did you really think I wouldn't?"

No. When he reached for her hand and wrapped his fingers around hers, she knew he would take on the devil himself to protect her—and very nearly had. If he'd jumped in front of her five seconds earlier, if Sherm Clark had realized eliminating her wouldn't have been a problem if he'd just killed Donovan first, he would be lying dead on the ground instead of holding her hand.

Tears welled in her eyes at the thought. "I could have lost you," she choked out.

Uncaring of the fact that her brother and Hunter were right there, listening to every word, he said, "That was never going to happen, sweetheart. Do you really think I'd let that bastard take me away from you? I love you. I'm not going anywhere without you."

"I think that's our cue to give you two some space," Hunter said with a grin.

"I hear the ambulances coming," Buck added, his blue eyes twinkling as his sister looked up at him, dazed. "The way I figure it, you've got ten minutes, tops, before you're both whisked back to the hospital and Donovan's operated on. After that, he's going to be so weak and drugged out, he won't know which end is up for at least forty-eight hours. If I were you, I'd talk fast."

Donovan gave Buck a sharp look. "I'm not playing games. I love her. Do you have any objections to that?"

"She's a grown woman and knows what she wants," her brother said. "If you haven't figured that out by now, you don't know her well enough to love her. Don't tell me. Tell her."

Grinning, Donovan turned back to Priscilla. "You heard him. I love you. Do you have any objections to that?"

"Just one," she murmured as she swayed toward him with a wicked grin. "What took you so long?"

Epilogue

Two Weeks Later

Harvey Pritchard was tall and as thin as a rail and could have passed for Jimmy Stewart. Pushing seventy, he was methodical and detail-oriented, and always on time. One year to the day after he'd first read the will to the Wyatts and made sure they understood the conditions of Hilda's will, he showed up at the Broken Arrow with paperwork for them to sign.

"Well, it looks like you all survived the year," he told them with a smile as he joined them in the family room. "Hilda would be proud of you. There was nothing she admired more than courage in the face of adversity."

"So she knew just about everyone in the county

would try to drive us away?" Katherine said, surprised. "She put us through all this on purpose?"

Sobering, he frowned. "I wouldn't say *on purpose,* no. But she felt it was important for you to know who your enemies were. And she wanted to make sure that you wanted the ranch badly enough to fight for it. From what I've heard, that's exactly what you've done."

"What about Sherm Clark?" Buck asked. "Was he telling the truth about Hilda being his mother or was that just a crazy lie he dreamed up to justify trying to kill us?"

Harvey hesitated, only to sigh. "When Sherm Clark tracked her down and demanded to know if she was his birth mother, she was shocked. She wanted nothing to do with him, nothing to do with the terrible memories she'd tried so hard to forget. She meant him no ill will, but she had no feelings for him. Considering the ordeal she went through, I don't think anyone can blame her for that."

"She was entitled to her feelings," Katherine said quietly. "She must have been horrified when he showed up on her doorstep and told her who he was."

"She had a very difficult time with it," the older man admitted. "I'd never seen her so distraught."

"If that was the case, then why did the sheriff think he was the unnamed heir?" Elizabeth asked, puzzled. "Surely, he could see how she felt."

"The man's crazy," Donovan said flatly. "He seemed to have this fantasy that because Hilda was his birthmother, he was a Wyatt and she really wanted him to have the Broken Arrow. It didn't seem to enter his head that she'd have left it to him outright if that was the case."

Remembering the fury in Sherm Clark's eyes, Priscilla shuddered and was thankful for the reassuring warmth and comfort of Donovan's arm around her shoulders. "Maybe he thought she left the place to us because we're the last of the legitimate heirs, but she really wanted him to have it."

"It's easy to see why he would think that," Buck added. "She left a loophole for an unnamed heir, and in his twisted mind, he deduced that it had to be him. If we didn't meet the conditions of the will, then the ranch would still go to a Wyatt."

"Even if it was one who was conceived as a result of a rape, then given up for adoption," Elizabeth said dryly. "Of course, the sheriff didn't see anything wrong with that. He just wanted the ranch and was willing to do just about anything to get it."

"And was the sheriff the unnamed heir?" Katherine asked Harvey Pritchard. "Or did he do all this for nothing?"

"I don't know," the attorney replied. "Hilda wrote the letter herself, and as far as I know, she never confided who the unnamed heir was to anyone. She certainly didn't tell me. And now that the conditions of the will have been met, and the paperwork completed, giving the four of you full ownership of the ranch, I see no reason why we can't open the letter and find out."

And with no further ado, he pulled out the letter that had caused so much trouble over the course of the past year and broke the seal on the back. Pulling out the short missive written entirely in Hilda's handwriting, the attorney read, "To whom it may concern. In the event that Buck, Elizabeth, Katherine, and Priscilla

Wyatt do not meet the conditions of my will, I hereby bequeath the Broken Arrow Ranch to the University of Colorado Department of Anthropology."

For a moment, there was nothing but stunned silence. Then Buck laughed. "Well, I'll be damned."

"The University of Colorado," Elizabeth said, frowning. "Why…oh my God, the Indians! She wanted the university to excavate the springs!"

"I should have guessed," the attorney said, chuckling. "She loved the ranch, loved the history of it, and was always intrigued with the Indians who lived here long before the Wyatts ever moved to Colorado. I'm not surprised that she would have left the Broken Arrow to the University if you'd decided you didn't want to leave England in order to meet the terms of the will."

"So the sheriff could have killed us all," Elizabeth's fiancé, John, said, "and he still wouldn't have gotten his hands on the ranch."

"And neither would the rest of the local bozos who thought they were the unnamed heir," Elizabeth retorted. "They did everything they could to make our lives a living hell, and all they're going to get for it is a rap sheet."

"So the rumors I've been hearing are true?" Harvey said. "Sherm Clark kept a record on his home computer of all the attacks on you and the ranch and who did what?"

Buck nodded grimly. "Apparently so. The FBI found the files when they searched his house. He planned to use them for a plea bargain if anyone ever discovered he was behind the more serious attacks."

"What a moron," Donovan said. "Now the FBI has

his files and enough evidence to arrest not only him, but Judge Garrison, the mayor, the county tax assessor and at least five neighbors."

"And the sheriff's claiming insanity," Katherine said. "Yeah, right. He's crazy, all right. Crazy like a fox."

"And desperate," Harvey said. "Prison isn't a nice place for former law enforcement officers. For some reason, the other inmates have it in for them." Smiling slightly, he snapped his briefcase shut and rose to his feet. "I know it's been rough, but the ranch is yours now. Enjoy it," he said as he shook hands all the way around. "You all earned it. Hilda would be pleased."

Just that simply, it was over. With his leave-taking, they all looked at each other and grinned. "How about some champagne?" Buck asked with a grin.

Just that quickly, the party began. The women quickly collected champagne glasses for everyone while Buck and John produced the champagne they'd put on ice earlier. Corks popped, the champagne flowed, and within minutes, they were all raising their glasses.

"To the Broken Arrow Ranch!"

"To Hilda!"

"To us!"

"To us!" Donovan repeated, and pulled Priscilla to his side for a kiss.

When he let her up for air, tears filled her eyes as she saw the love in his. "I love you," she said huskily. "I won't ever do to you what Jennifer did."

"I know that, sweetheart," he murmured, kissing her again. "I would never have asked you to marry me if I hadn't known I could trust you completely."

"Hummpph!" Buck said, clearing his throat. "It seems like there's another announcement to be made."

Blinking back tears, Priscilla turned to find the entire family grinning at them. "Oops." She laughed, and held out her hand and the diamond engagement ring that sparkled on her finger. "We're getting married!"

"Oh, my God! Why didn't you tell us? That's wonderful!"

"We can have a triple wedding!"

That drew a laugh from everyone as they surged forward to congratulate the two of them. They were passed from one family member to the next for hugs and kisses and pats on the back, and everyone was talking at once. It was Buck, however, who asked the question everyone else was thinking. "So where are you going to live since your job takes you all over the world?"

"We haven't even talked about that," Priscilla said. "With everything that's been going on, we haven't had time to work out any details. There's always London, of course. And Donovan has a place in San Diego—"

"Actually," Donovan replied, "I'm going to give up the bounty hunting."

Surprised, she blinked. "You are?"

"I've been giving it a lot of thought," he told her, "and I've been thinking of going back into law enforcement."

The announcement caught her totally off guard. "And you don't think we should have discussed this?" she asked, frowning.

"Not really," he said with a grin. "I thought you'd be pleased."

"Pleased?"

Her tone was anything but that, and he almost

laughed. "Well, yeah," he said with feigned innocence. "The Willow Bend Sheriff's office is looking for a sheriff, but if you don't want me to apply…"

For a moment, his announcement was met with nothing but silence. Then Priscilla laughed in delight and threw herself into his arms. "Are you serious? That's perfect! You've got to apply!"

"Good," he said, "because I already have. So start making plans to shut down your flat in London, sweetheart. I got the job!"

* * * * *

*Celebrate 60 years of pure reading pleasure
with Harlequin® Books!*

*Harlequin Romance® is celebrating by showering
you with DIAMOND BRIDES in February 2009.
Six stories that promise to bring a touch of sparkle
to your life, with diamond proposals and dazzling
weddings, sparkling brides and gorgeous grooms!*

*Enjoy a sneak peek at Caroline Anderson's
TWO LITTLE MIRACLES,
available February 2009
from Harlequin Romance®*

'I've found her.'

Max froze.

It was what he'd been waiting for since June, but now—now he was almost afraid to voice the question. His heart stalling, he leaned slowly back in his chair and scoured the investigator's face for clues. 'Where?' he asked, and his voice sounded rough and unused, like a rusty hinge.

'In Suffolk. She's living in a cottage.'

Living. His heart crashed back to life, and he sucked in a long, slow breath. All these months he'd feared—

'Is she well?'

'Yes, she's well.'

He had to force himself to ask the next question. 'Alone?'

The man paused. 'No. The cottage belongs to a man called John Blake. He's working away at the moment, but he comes and goes.'

God. He felt sick. So sick he hardly registered the next few words, but then gradually they sank in. 'She's got *what?*'

'Babies. Twin girls. They're eight months old.'

'Eight—?' he echoed under his breath. 'They must be his.'

He was thinking out loud, but the P.I. heard and corrected him.

'Apparently not. I gather they're hers. She's been there since mid-January last year, and they were born during the summer—June, the woman in the post office thought. She was more than helpful. I think there's been a certain amount of speculation about their relationship.'

He'd just bet there had. God, he was going to kill her. Or Blake. Maybe both of them.

'Of course, looking at the dates, she was presumably pregnant when she left you, so they could be yours, or she could have been having an affair with this Blake character before...'

He glared at the unfortunate P.I. 'Just stick to your job. I can do the math,' he snapped, swallowing the unpalatable possibility that she'd been unfaithful to him before she'd left. 'Where is she? I want the address.'

'It's all in here,' the man said, sliding a large envelope across the desk to him. 'With my invoice.'

'I'll get it seen to. Thank you.'

'If there's anything else you need, Mr Gallagher, any further information—'

'I'll be in touch.'

'The woman in the post office told me Blake was away at the moment, if that helps,' he added quietly, and opened the door.

Max stared down at the envelope, hardly daring to open it, but when the door clicked softly shut behind the P.I., he eased up the flap, tipped it and felt his breath jam in his throat as the photos spilled out over the desk.

Oh, lord, she looked gorgeous. Different, though. It took him a moment to recognise her, because she'd grown her hair, and it was tied back in a ponytail, making her look younger and somehow freer. The blond highlights were gone, and it was back to its natural soft golden-brown, with a little curl in the end of the ponytail that he wanted to thread his finger through and tug, just gently, to draw her back to him.

Crazy. She'd put on a little weight, but it suited her. She looked well and happy and beautiful, but oddly, considering how desperate he'd been for news of her for the past year—one year, three weeks and two days, to be exact—it wasn't only Julia who held his attention after the initial shock. It was the babies sitting side by side in a supermarket trolley. Two identical and absolutely beautiful little girls.

* * * * *

When Max Gallagher hires a P.I. to find his estranged wife, Julia, he discovers she's not alone—she has twin baby girls, and they might be his. Now workaholic Max has just two weeks to prove that he can be a wonderful husband and father to the family he wants to treasure.

Look for
TWO LITTLE MIRACLES
by Caroline Anderson,
available February 2009
from Harlequin Romance®

CELEBRATE
60 YEARS
OF PURE READING PLEASURE
WITH HARLEQUIN®!

We'll be spotlighting a different series
every month throughout 2009
to celebrate our 60th anniversary.

Look for Harlequin® Romance in February!

Harlequin® Romance is celebrating by showering
you with Diamond Brides in February 2009.

Six stories that promise to bring a touch of sparkle to
your life, with diamond proposals and dazzling weddings,
sparkling brides and gorgeous grooms!

Collect all six books in February 2009,
featuring *Two Little Miracles* by Caroline Anderson.

*Look for the Diamond Brides miniseries
in February 2009!*

www.eHarlequin.com   HRBRIDES09

HARLEQUIN® *Romance*®

This February the Harlequin® Romance series
will feature six Diamond Brides stories featuring
diamond proposals and gorgeous grooms.

Share your dream wedding proposal and you could WIN!

The most romantic entry will win a diamond
necklace and will inspire a proposal in one of
our upcoming Diamond Grooms books in 2010.

In 100 words or less, tell us the most romantic
way that you dream of being proposed to.

For more information, and to enter
the Diamond Brides Proposal contest, please visit
www.DiamondBridesProposal.com

Or mail your entry to us at:

IN THE U.S.: 3010 Walden Ave., P.O. Box 9069, Buffalo, NY 14269-9069
IN CANADA: 225 Duncan Mill Road, Don Mills, ON M3B 3K9

REQUEST YOUR FREE BOOKS!

2 FREE NOVELS PLUS 2 FREE GIFTS!

Silhouette® Romantic

SUSPENSE

Sparked by Danger, Fueled by Passion!

YES! Please send me 2 FREE Silhouette® Romantic Suspense novels and my 2 FREE gifts (gifts are worth about $10). After receiving them, if I don't wish to receive any more books, I can return the shipping statement marked "cancel." If I don't cancel, I will receive 4 brand-new novels every month and be billed just $4.24 per book in the U.S. or $4.99 per book in Canada, plus 25¢ shipping and handling per book plus applicable taxes, if any*. That's a savings of at least 15% off the cover price! I understand that accepting the 2 free books and gifts places me under no obligation to buy anything. I can always return a shipment and cancel at any time. Even if I never buy another book from Silhouette, the two free books and gifts are mine to keep forever.

240 SDN EEX6   340 SDN EEYJ

Name	(PLEASE PRINT)

Address	Apt. #

City	State/Prov.	Zip/Postal Code

Signature (if under 18, a parent or guardian must sign)

Mail to the **Silhouette Reader Service**:
IN U.S.A.: P.O. Box 1867, Buffalo, NY 14240-1867
IN CANADA: P.O. Box 609, Fort Erie, Ontario L2A 5X3

Not valid to current subscribers of Silhouette Romantic Suspense books.

Want to try two free books from another line?
Call 1-800-873-8635 or visit www.morefreebooks.com.

* Terms and prices subject to change without notice. N.Y. residents add applicable sales tax. Canadian residents will be charged applicable provincial taxes and GST. Offer not valid in Quebec. This offer is limited to one order per household. All orders subject to approval. Credit or debit balances in a customer's account(s) may be offset by any other outstanding balance owed by or to the customer. Please allow 4 to 6 weeks for delivery. Offer available while quantities last.

Your Privacy: Silhouette is committed to protecting your privacy. Our Privacy Policy is available online at www.eHarlequin.com or upon request from the Reader Service. From time to time we make our lists of customers available to reputable third parties who may have a product or service of interest to you. If you would prefer we not share your name and address, please check here. ☐

SRS08R

You're invited to join our Tell Harlequin Reader Panel!

By joining our new reader panel you will:

- Receive Harlequin® books—they are FREE and yours to keep with no obligation to purchase anything!
- Participate in fun online surveys
- Exchange opinions and ideas with women just like you
- Have a say in our new book ideas and help us publish the best in women's fiction

In addition, you will have a chance to win great prizes and receive special gifts! See Web site for details. Some conditions apply. Space is limited.

To join, visit us at

www.TellHarlequin.com.

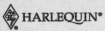

n o c t u r n e™

USA TODAY bestselling author

MAUREEN CHILD

VANISHED

Guardians

Immortal Guardian Rogan Butler
had no use for love, especially after his
Destined Mate abandoned him. So when beautiful
mortal Allison Blair sought his help against a
rising evil force, Rogan was bewildered by the
undeniable electric connection between them.
Besides, his true love had died years ago,
and it was impossible that he could even
have another Destined Mate—wasn't it?

Available February 2009 wherever books are sold.

www.eHarlequin.com
www.paranormalromanceblog.wordpress.com

Silhouette®
Romantic
SUSPENSE

COMING NEXT MONTH

#1547 SCANDAL IN COPPER LAKE—Marilyn Pappano
When Anamaria Duquesne returns to Copper Lake to discover the truth about her mother's death and her still-missing baby sister, she doesn't count on running into Robbie Calloway. Suspecting her of being a con artist, Robbie agrees to keep an eye on Anamaria, but he can't help entertaining feelings for her. And a relationship with Anamaria would be anything but easy....

#1548 A HERO OF HER OWN—Carla Cassidy
The Coltons: Family First
From the moment she arrives in town, Jewel Mayfair catches the attention of veterinarian Quinn Logan. They're both overcoming tragic pasts, but as Jewel lets down her guard to give in to passion with Quinn, mysterious events make her question her choices. Should she take a second chance on love, or is Quinn the last man she should trust?

#1549 THE REDEMPTION OF RAFE DIAZ—Maggie Price
Dates with Destiny
Businesswoman Allie Fielding never thought she'd see Rafe Diaz again—at least not on the outside of a prison cell! But when Allie stumbles over the body of a murdered customer, the now-exonerated P.I. she helped put behind bars shows up to question her. His investigation stirs up a past Rafe thought was behind him—and unlocks a passion that could put them both at risk.

#1550 HEART AT RISK—Ana Leigh
Bishop's Heroes
A family was the furthest thing from Kurt Bolen's mind, yet when he discovers he has a son, he'll do whatever it takes to make the boy and his mother his own. But someone is after Kurt, and in the midst of rekindling their romance, he and Maddie must band together to protect their son and fight for their future.